Beyond
Church Doors

D1105115

Beyond Church Doors

✦ A NOVEL ✦

Sylvia Brown-Roberts

iUniverse, Inc.
Bloomington

Beyond Church Doors

iUniverse books may be ordered through booksellers or by contacting:

iUniverse
1663 Liberty Drive
Bloomington, IN 47403
www.iuniverse.com
1-800-Authors (1-800-288-4677)

ISBN: 978-1-4759-6871-2 (sc)
ISBN: 978-1-4759-6873-6 (hc)
ISBN: 978-1-4759-6872-9 (ebk)

Library of Congress Control Number: 2013900218

Printed in the United States of America

iUniverse rev. date: 01/17/2013

Acknowledgements

I give thanks to God.
I thank all of you.

Sylvia Brown-Roberts
Website: www.nikkimacproductions.com

Table of Contents

Introduction

My name is Nikolis McQuaige and I'm a Christian. Most people call me NikkiMac. I'm called a redbone because of my light skin and red hair. My face showcases brown freckles, especially on my cheeks and across my nose. I'm a curvy woman with a small waistline. The needle on my home scale dances around 150 pounds. I'm 40 years old and single, but not necessarily single by choice. However, I've pretty much stopped searching for love. My energy is now spent on living a faithful life in Christ. Although I'm not an angel, I've been blessed by God to make improvements in my life. Take men, for example. My last relationship was with Alex Carson, and it ended when I began to feel guilty about our casual, mutual, and friendly intimacy. I allowed Alex to become a friend with benefits. Later, when I became a Christian, I couldn't convince him that God sanctions such intimacy only in marriage. As a result, he ended our friendship.

I teach in an elementary public school in the city of Trenton, New Jersey, and my best friend is Jacee Fontinetta Jackson. She's my petite, chocolate, and feisty cut buddy. Jacee teaches in the school system, too. She's also a member of the church. We've been friends since we met in elementary school. We grew up in the same neighborhood, and attended Junior High School Number One, Trenton High School and Rutgers University together. The two of us have been close for so long that when I show up someplace without Jacee, at least one person always asks where she is, or how she's doing. The same thing happens to Jacee when she shows up someplace without me. I love her like a sister.

Anna Maria DelGrosso is a new friend. She works as a secretary at my school. She's one of those on-point people. If you ever tell her you need something done, be prepared for her to jump right on it. If you want to think about it for a minute before you act, don't tell Anna Maria until you're absolutely ready to start. Anna Maria is what we call good people. She is all about "just the facts" but she has a heart of gold. She does plenty of nice things for folks, but she never mentions this. I usually hear about her kindness from the people who've received it. She doesn't like to talk about her acts of benevolence.

My parents died when I was in my twenties. I still live in their house, not too far from the train freight yard. I enjoy this old house with its many memories of my mom, Alice McQuaige, and my dad, Nickson McQuaige. It's been a long time since they've passed on, but I still miss them so much.

My father figure by choice is an older man I call Poppa Pace. His proper name is Foster Pace. He's a faithful Christian brother who has looked out for me since I met him. He rescued me one night when I was somewhere I shouldn't have been, and he invited me to a church service. I accepted his invitation and was later added to the church. For several years, I've been part of this lively church family in Trenton, New Jersey. I'm also a resident of the urban neighborhood where the church meets. Cletus, who used to be the neighborhood drunk, is now a close friend as well as my brother in Christ. I still put up with Tasha Pace, the wayward daughter of my Poppa Pace, but I honestly admit that I don't have the agape Christian love for her that I should have. Darius Muse, the man who attempted an assault on me years ago and was interrupted by Poppa Pace, is now a member of the church. I greet Darius at church, but I don't have much else to say to him. There are a couple of other people that get on my nerves, but for the most part, I try to get along with everyone. I don't want or need drama. My faith is a serious matter to me, but I confess to weakness in some areas. I get tempted. At times, I have a quick tongue. Sometimes, I allow my thoughts to stray where they shouldn't. I mess up every now and then. However, I'm getting better about allowing God to help me improve. That way, I can be what He wants me to be in this life. I'm a work in progress.

Chapter 1

Is It Just My Imagination?

What's wrong with me? Why can't I fall asleep tonight? I hate it when this happens! I climbed into my queen-sized bed at 10:00, and now the red digital numbers on my bedside clock shout that it's almost 11:15. I've prepared for sleep. I've tried all my favorite slumber positions, but none of them have worked their magic. Covers on, covers off, I've done that routine. My feet have even searched for the cool spots in my bed, a trick that usually works to start my dream journey. Except for slivers of the streetlight's glow that slip through the miniblinds, my bedroom is dark. The room temperature is just right. I've said my prayers. Wait, here it comes. My eyelids begin to shut down; the sense of drifting is finally here.

In my dream, I smell frankincense. I see myself in my bed. The dark figure of a man sits on the side of my bed, and he looks down at me. I feel his warm, strong hands. They make a steady rhythm, a kneading rhythm. This is not a sexual touch; it's soothing. His hands rub my neck and shoulders, my outer arms, and travel down to my lower back. The hands stop there. Then, the pattern repeats: neck, shoulders, arms, and lower back. I'm not afraid. I feel protected. I hear his whispery voice say, "Everything's gonna be alright, Nikolis. It's okay, Baby Girl. Sleep. Sleep on. I've got you."

Initially, there is peace. Briefly after that, an ominous sense startles me from this dreamy state to consciousness. Suddenly, I sit up! Is that a sound downstairs? Is someone on the staircase? Did I really feel those hands rub my body? Was there actually someone here with me? I rub my eyes and shake my head. My heartbeat bangs in my ears. One minute, I'm in a soothing dream. The next minute, I'm scared that an intruder is in my house! I grab my baseball bat from under the bed and race downstairs, all the while praying, "Lord, please help me. Please protect me!" I turn on the lights and check the front door. It's locked, and so are the living room and dining room windows. Everything looks okay so far. My feet carry me quickly to the kitchen and the back door. Things in here seem normal. The door still appears locked like when I checked it before bed, but my hands jiggle the handle anyway. The door opens! I know I locked this back door! I'm anal about locking my windows and doors before turning in for the night. My brain scrambles while my fingers lock the door and my eyes peek through its small windowpane. My eyes scan the back yard and the fence. No one is in my yard, but I think I see a shadow moving on the other side of my back fence. Yes, there's a figure moving down the alley between Poplar Street and Hart Avenue.

Once more, I smell frankincense, like in my dream earlier. I sniff my right shoulder. The aroma is on me, but I didn't put any of the fragrant oil on my body before bed. Was someone in my home? Was someone in my bedroom touching me? Maybe I wasn't dreaming after all.

I turn on all the lights on the first floor and sit in the chair nearest the front door, armed with my bat and now a kitchen knife. My first thought is to call my best friend, Jacee, but why wake her up at this time of night? She's alone at her place just like I'm alone here. Rational thinking returns and I call 911, and pace while I wait for the Trenton police to arrive.

Within a few minutes, they show up. I peek through the window while they park their black and white cruiser, get out, and walk up my front steps. When I open the door, it makes me feel good to recognize one of the two men. It's Brother Sampson, a member of the church and a Trenton police officer.

"Sister NikkiMac, what's up? We got a call about a possible intruder here. Are you okay?" I'm so relieved to see him that I almost hug him, but respect his official capacity and shake his hand instead. He's over six feet tall and carries at least two hundred seventy-five pounds on his thick frame. He has a sense of humor, but he doesn't take any mess from folks. He's a hard worker at church and he commands respect in his job. His expression is filled with concern for me.

"Brother Sampson, I'm so glad to see you!" He introduces me to his partner, Officer Suarez, and they come inside to listen to my account, but I omit the part about my dream. I'm not sure why I keep that part from them, though. I tell them about the noise I heard and the dark figure I saw. They check outside, even in the alley. Brother Sampson returns and observes me with a look of care.

"Sister NikkiMac, did you see any signs of forcible entry?"

"No. I believe I locked the back door before I went to bed, but when I got up to check on the noise, the door was closed, but it was unlocked."

Brother Sampson frowns ever so slightly and says, "Is that right? Sister NikkiMac, do you mind if we search inside your house?"

"No, I don't mind. Please do a search." All of a sudden, my knees get wobbly. Brother Sampson notices, and he gently helps me to the sofa. The officers search inside the house, open closet doors, and go through the basement. My attic is only a crawl space, but Officer Suarez scoots up there and checks it out. As they look around outside the house again, the beams from their flashlights pierce through the darkness. The officers return to the house and ask me more questions.

"Sister NikkiMac, does anyone else have a key to your back door? A relative, maybe?"

I turn my head from side to side while I answer Officer Sampson, "No."

"An angry boyfriend, perhaps?" Officer Suarez asks delicately.

I flash my eyes and reply, "Absolutely not! Officer Suarez, I live alone, and I don't have a boyfriend. Even if I did have a boyfriend, he wouldn't have a key to my house."

Brother Sampson looks sharply at his partner and speaks softly through clenched teeth, "Man, I told you she was a good Christian woman."

"I didn't mean any disrespect, Miss McQuaige. I'm trying to figure out how the door that you locked got unlocked. Sometimes people leave a spare key with a neighbor and it gets into the wrong hands. Sometimes a purse gets stolen with the house keys and ID inside. You didn't say anything about these two things earlier, so I asked about a boyfriend because I'm trying to cover all bases." Since Officer Suarez shows clear concern for my situation, I bring my attitude back in check.

Brother Sampson turns to me, "Sister NikkiMac, we checked the alley, your carport, yard and garden areas, and we didn't see any evidence of someone being on your property outside, but it is dark out there. We'll swing by here on our patrols tonight and keep an eye out. This is my cell number. Use it if you need to, Sister." He hands me an official business card. I grab my cell phone right then and enter the cell number in my contacts list. Before the two officers leave, we all double-check my doors and windows.

"Thank you so much, officers. I really appreciate you for not treating me like a crazy woman who sees things that aren't there."

"Sister NikkiMac, I've known you and your work in the church long enough to confirm your sanity. If you suspect something isn't right, it needs to be checked out. That's our job." Brother Sampson gives me a friendly wink. Officer Suarez nods his head in agreement.

"Thanks again, officers." I close the door, lock it, and watch them until they drive away. Not even bothering to go back upstairs to my bed, I get some blankets and a spare pillow from the linen closet. I keep all the first floor lights on. Then, I make a cup of ginger tea. A click of the remote turns on the television. Its soft background noise reassures me. The sofa makes a comfy retreat for my spirit and body. I place my baseball bat, cell phone, and my knife where I can quickly reach them. I sip the tea and give thanks and pray to God for His peace and protection. Eventually, I feel sleep come my way. My last view before slumber is of the clock on the wall with its hands positioned at 12:55. It is officially Sunday morning. My eyes close.

When I open them later, the clock reads 8 o'clock in the morning. I briefly wonder why I'm downstairs on the sofa instead of upstairs in my bed. "What in the world?" I say out loud. Then, I remember last night. The knife, my cell phone, and the baseball bat rest near me. I bow my head and pray. "Thank you, heavenly Father, for watching over me last night, and for waking me up this morning." Just hearing my voice say the words gives me courage, and I check the two doors and the windows. Everything is the same as when I fell asleep. My feet carry me upstairs, where I search every room before slipping out of my pajamas and stepping into the shower. I leave the shower curtain open a little, because the well-known shower scene from Alfred Hitchcock's *Psycho* pops into my head. I chase the vision away and alter my thoughts so I don't jump out of my skin.

I've lived here alone for many years, and this is the first time I've ever experienced a feeling of danger while in this house. I finish getting dressed. Then, I reach for my small ring box that I keep on the table next to my bed. The box holds a cherished ring that my late parents gave me. Every morning after getting dressed, I take out my blue chalcedony ring, place it on the third finger of my right hand, and kiss the stone in memory of my parents. Something's strange, though. The ring is on the table, but the ring box is missing. I look under the bed while I run scenarios through my head about the ring's place on the table without the ring box. This doesn't make sense to me at all, but I'll have to figure it out later. Right now, I'm ready to be with my fellow Christians. Except for Poppa Pace, Jacee, and Brother Sampson, I don't want to talk to anyone about my experience last night. First, I need to process this, because I don't think I'm crazy, and I don't want anyone to think my imagination is running wild. I also don't want well meaning but alarmist people to make me afraid to live alone. I eat some oatmeal with raisins. I check my doors and windows again, grab my Bible and my purse, leave my house, and drive to the church building. On the way, I sing *His Eye Is On The Sparrow.*

Chapter 2

New Converts Reception

In spite of last night's events, I arrive at the church building with a sense of calm. Jacee meets me on the church steps.

"Good morning, NikkiMac. You look a little tired today. How was your evening?"

"I knew you'd notice, Jacee. I did have a weird experience last night. I thought I heard a noise in the house, and I thought I saw someone running in the alley behind the house, so I called the police." I try to make this sound light so Jacee doesn't stress, but it doesn't work. Jacee stops in her tracks and grabs me by the elbow.

"What do you mean? Somebody broke into your house! Did the police catch him?" Her hazel eyes flash with alarm, and her voice booms.

"Jacee, calm down! Brother Sampson and his partner came right away. They searched and didn't find anyone. Brother Sampson even gave me his direct contact number so I can reach him if I have any more problems, so I feel better. To be honest with you, Jacee, I think I had a crazy dream and I might have imagined things, even the noise."

"But what about the person you saw in the alley?"

"Jacee, you and I both know that folks still travel through that alley to get into their backyards and to their back doors. Maybe one of those teenaged girls on Hart Avenue or Poplar Street told her boyfriend to slip out the back way because her parents were coming in the front door!" I force a smile, but Jacee doesn't return it. Instead, she stares at me for a minute before she speaks.

"Well, thank God you're okay, but we'll talk more about this after church. Did you tell Brother Pace? What did he say?"

"No, Jacee. I called him this morning, and we'll talk after church."

"Well, I plan to be in on the conversation, Miss McQuaige." When she calls me by my last name, it means her mind is made up. I realize that we're a little late for worship service, so we enter the church building and find our seats. The song leader moves through the fourth verse of *Lord, Send Me*, and then Minister Obadiah Johnson stands before the congregation.

"Good morning, brothers, sisters, and visiting friends. It's a privilege to see you this Sunday morning. Every Lord's Day is special, and we're instructed by God to meet collectively for worship. This particular Sunday is special to our congregation for another reason: we're going to recognize our members who've been baptized this year. It's all about encouraging them in their walk of faith."

"Amen, Brother Johnson!"

"That's right!"

"The idea for this Sunday program came from Sister NikkiMac, one of our hard workers in the programs for children. Sometimes people who are longtime members of the church forget that new converts often face strong challenges. This is especially true if those new converts are the only ones in their households who are in the church. It can be difficult as new members move from one way of life to another, and we old-timers would do well to remember that fact. Today, at the end of worship service, we're going to have a New Converts Reception in the dining hall. Please stay for a few minutes, have some light refreshments, and get to know some of our newest members of the congregation. I challenge you to find out one thing you didn't know about each of our ten new members." He asks the ushers to distribute index cards with the names of the ten members on each of them. Underneath each name is a blank space for us to record one fact we discover about the member. Brother Johnson instructs us to keep these cards and use them as a springboard for becoming better acquainted.

"This should be fun, NikkiMac," says Jacee. I'm glad I have her as a life friend as well as a Christian sister. Brother Johnson reads the names of the new converts and asks them to stand.

"New members, please stand so we all can see who you are. We're doing this at the start of service because some folks leave right after they take communion. Don't think I don't notice that some of you regularly slip out of the auditorium before service is over, but that's a topic for another Sunday."

"That's all right, preacher!"

"Say it, Brother Johnson!"

"This is Sister Chloe Shasheem. She was baptized recently after a Sunday evening service." Chloe stands up quickly. She's a slim, tall, and shapely woman, with a short haircut and eyes shaped like almonds. Her skin is the color of a ripe Georgia peach and her jet-black hair looks straight and silky. Her remarkable eyes flash instead of gaze. She doesn't smile, but she does give a brief wave before she sits back down.

"Jacee, I haven't noticed her here before, have you?"

"No, I can't say that I have, NikkiMac. Why?"

"She looks about our age and she looks interesting, that's why. Oh, you know what? You and I were at that weekend conference in Baltimore recently and we attended church there. That's probably when Sister Chloe was baptized here. We need to make sure we introduce ourselves to Sister Chloe at the reception this afternoon."

"Whatever, NikkiMac, but she doesn't seem all that friendly. Would it have hurt her to smile when she stood up just now?" I look closely at Jacee to see if she's kidding, but her facial expression says she's not. Her hazel eyes darken and she pats her fluffy Afro.

After our minister has the ten new converts stand to be recognized, the song leader comes forward to direct *Holy, Holy, Holy*. We continue with scripture reading and sing two more hymns before the selected brothers come to the communion table for the Lord's Supper. Prayer is offered, and after all members of the church are served the unleavened crackers and the grape juice, Brother Vonner leads us in singing *How Great Thou Art*. Our minister then enters the pulpit to deliver the sermon.

"You all know I'm not the best singer in the church, but it's okay with the Lord because I sing from my heart. I want you to sing *Never Alone* with me, church, because that's the theme for my sermon this morning. Is that all right with you all?"

"Amen! Amen!"

"Sing, Brother Johnson!"

Our minister clears his throat and starts off the song. He's right, he's certainly not the best singer, but sincerity can be heard in his strong voice. We join him and sing all four verses of the hymn with gusto. "Thank you for singing with me. The words to that hymn connect with the scripture found in Hebrews chapter 13, verses 5 and 6. Please find these verses in your Bibles." The rustle of the turning pages is a familiar sound.

"These verses remind us that God is always with His children. In good and bad times, when there's peace and when there's trouble, when there's joy and when there's sadness, He is always with us. That should give us comfort and faithful confidence! That should keep us away from depression! When we fully put our trust in God, we embrace His presence. We walk daily like we *know* He's taking care of all that concerns us! Y'all don't hear me, church!"

"We hear you! Amen!"

"Preach, preacher!"

"Glory!"

Brother Johnson preaches for a short while longer, and then we stand for the invitation song. No one walks forward to be added to the church, so the ushers collect the offering and a brother offers a prayer of thanksgiving. Another brother reads the announcements, and then Brother Sampson leads us in a closing prayer.

"Amen," repeats the congregation after the prayer. I greet church members quickly, because I want to get to the dining hall to speak with the new converts. Except for Sister Chloe and an older sister, I remember witnessing their baptisms. I think Brother Johnson introduced the cute, petite older woman this morning as Sister Lovey Grace, but I'm not sure I heard her name correctly.

"NikkiMac, do you have your index card for the reception activity?" Jacee asks.

"Yes. Come on, let's find a seat."

The chairs in the dining hall have been arranged in a large circle. After we take our seats, our minister offers a prayer.

"Our heavenly Father, we thank you for this opportunity to celebrate our newest members of the body of Christ. Please bless these babes in Christ with the strength to resist the evil one and the desire to do Your will. Please encourage the other members of the congregation to reach out to the new converts and support them in their walk of faith. Please help us all remember that we must study the Bible, pray, and yield to the Holy Spirit in order to live in a way that pleases you. Thank you, Father. In the name of Jesus we pray. Amen."

"Amen," the congregation responds.

"Members of the Sisters Bible Class have prepared a nice spread of cheese and crackers, some fruit trays, and some fruit juices. We also have coffee and tea service, and containers of delicious spring water. Please enjoy the refreshments. Just remember, our purpose is to get to know our new members. Take out your index cards and start greeting folks!" Minister Johnson takes out his card and walks over to a new brother, shakes his hand, and begins a conversation. I look at Sister Chloe, who appears to be bored by this activity.

"Jacee, I'm going to introduce myself to Sister Chloe. Come go with me."

"For what, NikkiMac? She looks like she doesn't even want to be here. I'm going over to meet that young married couple. They seem friendly." Jacee walks to another part of the circle.

I cut my eyes at Jacee's back, and then walk over to Sister Chloe. As much as I hate to admit it, Jacee's right on point. Sister Chloe's piercing dark eyes send out unfriendly rays, but I'm already in motion, so I don't let that stop me.

"Hi, my name is Sister Nikolis McQuaige, but most people call me Sister NikkiMac. I'm very pleased to meet you. Welcome to the congregation, Sister Chloe." I lean in to touch her cheek against mine in a warm gesture of greeting, but she rears her head back and instead sticks her gloved hand out for a handshake.

"I don't do the cheek touch thing, and I don't usually shake hands, but since I'm wearing gloves today, I will. Thank you for your greeting, Sister McQuaige." Sister Chloe's voice is crisp, but her volume is soft. Her enunciated words are powerful, like slaps in the face. Her handshake is quite firm and her eyes stare directly at mine.

"What's wrong with a nude handshake, Sister Chloe? We greet each other that way here." My intent is to disarm her with a little humor.

"I don't shake hands without wearing gloves because it's a germy thing to do. Do you realize how many germs are on our hands? The Bible may tell us to greet each other, but we also have to be wise, Sister McQuaige."

Even though she looks at me like I have the cooties, I ignore her germ phobia and continue in a somewhat friendly tone. "You can call me Sister NikkiMac, like most people around here do." I smile, and take a seat next to Sister Chloe.

"I'm sure you'll find out that I'm not like most people, Sister McQuaige. Now, ask me your question so you can write a factoid about me on your index card. Then, you can move on to one of the other nine new members."

Before I can catch my thoughts, they fly to the front of my brain and almost out of my mouth. Who does this heifer think she is? I'm trying to be friendly! Thankfully, I check my tongue and ask, "So, where are you from, Sister Chloe? Are you originally from New Jersey?" I know my smile looks phony, but it's the best I can do. This woman's unprovoked behavior bewilders me.

"I'm from the planet Earth, Sister McQuaige. You've asked your question, so you may move on to another new member." She doesn't smile, yet she doesn't have an angry facial expression. It's a matter-of-fact look.

I can't resist. "Excuse me, do I know you from someplace else? You seem to have a problem with me. Or is it that you're just rude? Whatever your problem is, it's a good thing you came to church, because you truly need Jesus!"

Sister Chloe finally smiles and shows little pearly, perfectly shaped teeth. "Good day, Sister McQuaige. It's been real." She turns her back to me and engages in conversation with Sister Melody, who shows up all of a sudden.

"How perfect," I whisper to myself. "The two of them can have a Cutest Person Contest! I'm done with this chick!" In my haste to get away from Sister Chloe before I get her told and from Sister Melody before she gets her nosey on, I bump into Poppa Pace.

"Hello, Daughter NikkiMac. You look troubled. What's wrong?"

"Poppa Pace, please walk with me, because I'm about to burst!" I take his arm and we stride out of the dining hall.

"Calm down and tell me what's going on. Is it what you called me about this morning?" As usual, his composed voice and soothing manner begin to settle my spirit.

"No, Poppa Pace. We can have that conversation later. This is about Sister Chloe. I introduced myself to that woman and she was downright rude to me! She was so nasty to me, you'd think I stole something from her!"

Poppa Pace puts an arm around my shoulder. "Daughter NikkiMac, you know you haven't done anything bad to our new sister. You just met her. Who knows? Maybe you remind her of someone who mistreated her in her past. Obviously, the problem is within her. Just give it time and pray for her. Go back inside and meet the other new members, and I'll catch up with you later for our talk. Why not go over there and get acquainted with Sister Lovey Grace? I just spoke with her and she's quite pleasant. Meanwhile, I'll introduce myself to Sister Chloe. Maybe there's something I can do to help smooth her rough edges."

"Thanks, Poppa Pace. Good luck with that." I pat him on his shoulder and then return to the dining hall. I think I see him smile and shake his head, but I don't respond. I've got nine more members to meet, and I'm too busy mumbling, "Good luck with that mean-eyed heifer!"

Poppa Pace was right, as usual. Sister Lovey Grace and her welcoming manner are a delightful contrast to Sister Chloe. "I'm so glad to meet you, Sister NikkiMac. Thank you for coming over to speak with me." She extends both of her hands to hold mine, and I notice her attractive fingers and beautiful nails.

"You have lovely hands, Sister Grace. Your nails are well manicured. Do you have them done at a salon around here?"

"No, dear, I just file them myself. They're hard and they grow quickly. I simply file them each Saturday night and use clear nail polish on them. Thank you for the compliment, Sister NikkiMac." She smiles at me.

I show her my nails. "Well, I need to find out what kind of polish you use, because I work in the classroom with children and I'm constantly washing my hands or using hand sanitizer. As a result, my nails are always popping or splitting."

"I know what you mean, Sister NikkiMac. Before I retired, I worked with children, so I understand the wear and tear on your hands and nails. I keep mine moisturized, and I shape the tips in a slightly rounded fashion. I try to avoid filing my nails into sharp edges because they cause snagged ends. Here, let me look at your hands more closely." She examines them gently. She reminds me of an old-time southern schoolteacher: all bright-eyed smiles when students do their best, a raised eyebrow and pursed lips when they do nonsense. Sister Lovey

Grace's skin has the red undercoat of Native American ancestors mixed with African American ones. She has the faintest mustache, but on her, it looks sweet. We continue to chat. I forget all about Sister Chloe Shasheem and her funky attitude.

Chapter 3

Cletus and NikkiMac Go Downtown

Every now and then, a school closing gives me a day off from work, so I get to visit shops in downtown Trenton during the day, when plenty of people are around. Although much of downtown Trenton has deteriorated since I was a teenager, there are still some places of shopping interest. One of my favorite stores has quality body oils for sale. At least two other shops carry unique soaps, cosmetics, and skin care products. The prices for these items are quite reasonable. I don't buy hair or wigs, but many other local women do, and there's lots of hair for sale. Downtown Trenton hosts some boutiques, nail salons, good restaurants, and even a spa. There's the Sound of Trenton music store, Classics Bookstore, and the Peanut Shop. Some shops offer the latest in urban gear, jewelry, and music. Trenton is also the home of the historic Old Barracks Museum, the New Jersey State Museum, and the Planetarium. I routinely take my students on field trips to these educational and distinctive places that are so close to their West Trenton neighborhood. It amazes me when my students and other city residents admit they haven't been to these Trenton and New Jersey state treasures, or don't visit them often. Yet, on weekdays when school is in session, school buses from districts all over the state pull up in front of the Capital Complex.

Street parking in town is a pain I can live without. I think more folks would come downtown if they could drive in and park more easily. I don't like to use the parking lots. I think most of them are for the state workers or other people with permits. As a result, I usually end up driving past City Hall, where there are often no available metered parking spots. Next, I drive by the Broad Street Bank Building Apartments and the Post Office until I reach the light near the Mill Hill Theater. My usual strategy is to make a left turn at this light and find a parking spot near the Architects House. I follow that pattern today, but as I turn, I almost bump into Brother Cletus, who's crossing the street.

"Whoa! Can't you see I'm walking here?" Cletus hollers to me.

"Cletus, I'm so sorry! Are you okay?" I slam on the brakes before my car makes contact with his lanky body.

"NikkiMac, is that you? Are you trying to run a brother over with your car? You mad or something?" Cletus shouts and quickly moves to the curb, but he's smiling. I'm glad to see him.

"Wait, Cletus. I'm going to park by the Architects House and join you."

He laughs. "The way you're driving today, you probably *should* park that car and walk. That way, folks will be safer, my sister!"

After I park and put money in the parking meter, I cross the street and catch up with Cletus. He looks so much better since he became a member of the church and stopped drinking alcohol. He attends his AA meetings regularly. He takes care of his ailing elderly mother and helps Brother Pace with the church building's maintenance. That's what giving his life to Christ did for Cletus. I'm so proud of him. His transformation reminds me of how God's power can change lives.

"Let me apologize again, my brother. I truly didn't mean to startle you like that." Cletus and I give each other a friendly embrace.

"Apology accepted, NikkiMac. What brings you downtown today?"

"I want to get some body oils from the little shop on East State Street. Their oils are less expensive than at some other places I've found in the area. The quality is excellent and they have a wide selection. I like that you get to choose from three bottle sizes and prices: three dollars, five dollars, or ten dollars. The storeowner pours the oil from the large batch bottle right in front of the customer and he uses the roller ball heads on the bottles. That way, you can apply it to your skin easily, without wasting any oil."

"NikkiMac, you could do a commercial for the oil shop! You said all that without taking a breath! I had to come downtown to pay our Public Service bill. Mother doesn't believe in mailing it, so it's my job to come downtown and handle it for her. Come on, I'll walk with you. If I remember correctly, that shop carries my favorite hand and body lotion. You probably know which one I'm talking about. This company in Newark manufactures the lotion. I just used up my last bottle, so I need to buy some more. It's good stuff. It smells great, and it beats back ash better than any of the high-priced lotions I've used. It costs less downtown, and I can't find it at the major drugstores around here. Come to think of it, I don't think there are any major drugstore chains in downtown Trenton anymore. That's a shame."

"You're right about the drugstores, and I know the brand of lotion you mean, Cletus. It's an urban product, and often, you can't find it in mainstream brand stores. They should get better buyers, because we spend money for the products we like."

We laugh together and start walking toward East State Street. It's a pleasant and breezy day, so many people are out on the streets. At the top of the hill, we make a left onto East State Street and head in the direction of the State and Broad Street intersection. When we reach the old, inactive Trenton Saving Fund Society bank building, I notice the closed, locked metal gates and the old stone steps. Fond memories come to mind, memories of the Trenton public schools elementary banking program and of the yellow paper banking envelopes. In them, we placed the hard-earned nickels and dimes and quarters of our parents. I recall banking day being a weekly event, held each Thursday. We gave the yellow envelopes to our teachers and the envelopes were delivered to this Trenton Saving Fund Bank. On Monday, we got our bankbooks back and dutifully took them home to our parents, who kept them until the next banking Thursday. From a young age, many of us Trenton public school students learned to be savers. We were so proud when we reviewed our bankbooks, stamped with the slow but steadily growing amounts.

Today, there's a sad contrast to this once thriving bank in Trenton's downtown. A man who appears to be homeless sits in a faded lawn chair in front of the building's bottom step. He could be about fifty years old. The hairs on his head and in his beard are salt and pepper in color. The whites of his eyes are yellow, as are his teeth. The man's eyes watch us approach him. He sizes us up. He asks for money with a gruff, angry tone. "Got a dollar?"

I act like I don't hear the man, so Cletus answers, "Naw, man. I don't have a dollar for you today."

He snorts at Cletus before he responds. "My man, you come downtown and pass by me in this spot in front of this bank at least once a week and every time I ask you for a dollar, you say the same thing. When *are* you gonna have a dollar for me? That's what *I* wanna know!" I stifle a laugh and make my feet move faster, away from this beggar with a bad attitude. Cletus shakes his head and moves along with me down the street. We hear the same man ask, "Got a dollar?" to the people behind us.

Like many urban cities, downtown Trenton has its share of folks who take the bus or walk into town from their nearby neighborhoods. Today, the bus stop at State and Broad has about fifteen folks waiting outside the fast food chicken place.

"Cletus, do you remember that when we were in Trenton High School, this chicken place used to be a restaurant called La Petite? After school, we caught the bus from the high school on Chambers Street and got off here. Some of the kids waited here for a transfer to another bus. My crew would hang out downtown for awhile before we walked home to East Trenton."

"I remember, NikkiMac. If we were lucky enough to have some money, we'd go into La Petite and buy something to eat before walking home. Some kids caught the L-East Trenton bus home, if they could bum a bus transfer off somebody. I usually walked. Those were the days." Cletus has a dreamy look in his eyes.

"I know, Cletus. Jacee, me, and a couple of other girlfriends would go into La Petite, wait for a booth and determine if we had enough money to pay for our food and still leave a tip. There was an older waitress who made sure teenagers who tipped got a decent booth. My favorite order was the Cheeseburger Deluxe Platter: a large, hand-formed beef burger served open face on a bun with melted American cheese, a side of crispy fries, a cup of coleslaw, and half of a large dill pickle. I'd wash my meal down with a chocolate milkshake. The food was served on white porcelain plates, and they gave us real silverware, not plastic utensils. Plus, it only cost about two dollars and fifty cents for all that food! You couldn't tell us we weren't living large!" The nostalgia quiets us for a minute or two.

When we cross Broad Street, the crowd becomes thicker. There are people who work here along with the people who live here. The state workers are in groups, out for lunch. Their "safety in numbers strategy" is clearly evident. There are men dressed in suits. Others wear pressed slacks with shirts and ties. Women in dresses and pantsuits contrast with the females in pajama pants and hoodies. Many of the local guys wear jeans and sweatpants. A few of the waistbands on the jeans and the sweatpants hang low enough to reveal underwear and more. The style of dress and the demeanor clearly indicate which people work downtown or have legitimate business and those who are here to see what they can see. The floaters are here, too. Some of the floaters stand on the street corners and ask for cigarette money through clenched teeth, because they know the security people are watchful in this area these days. They have to be, since times have changed from the days when almost all Trenton folks hung out downtown for fun. Some of the floaters are on the lookout for personal opportunities that aren't so nice for the people on the other end. Other floaters slowly cruise by on old bicycles. They weave in and out of traffic. Their eyes are both streetwise and weary.

After I buy my aromatic oils in the shop, Cletus and I walk to the Trenton Downtown Hotel, where I offer to treat him to lunch. In the hotel restaurant, we try some delicious fruit drinks and then give our food orders to the waiter. Cletus clears his throat before he speaks. "NikkiMac, the good Lord must have meant for us to be together today, because you've been on my mind. There's something I want to talk to you about. I respect your opinion because you're an intelligent sister." He looks like he's about to sell me some snake oil, so I'm curious, but not concerned. Before Cletus became a Christian, he'd often hang out near the church building so he could bum money off me. He'd always use his corny charm first. Back then, my role in these interactions was to scold him because he never came into the church building to listen to the gospel. I'd even warn him about using the spare change I gave him to buy booze. It was our little dance. Although he was down and out then, we shared a type of respect for one another. My thoughts return to the present.

"What's up, Cletus?"

"NikkiMac, you know Angeleese comes to church pretty regular, right?" He doesn't wait for me to answer, so I don't. "She tells me that her twins, Mookie and Shay Shay, are my kids. I'm thinking about getting a paternity test to see what's what. If it turns out they're my kids, I've got to do something about it. I want to know, and besides, it's the Christian thing to do." He wears an expression of obligation, but I sense tenderness and a passion in his voice. I place my words carefully.

"Cletus, do you have romantic feelings for Angeleese?"

"I know I feel something more than *like* for her, NikkiMac. She may be a little different, but she's as sweet as they come. She loves her children, and takes better care of them than many mothers I've seen."

I blink, and then speak. "Cletus, I hear what you're saying, but remember, Angeleese has three other children and each one has a different father. Do you want to date and maybe eventually marry a woman with intellectual disabilities, with all that baggage? Can you afford to support her and those five children? Face the facts: you live with your elderly mother and Angeleese lives with her elderly grandmother. Plus, even though Angeleese comes to church now, she's afraid to get baptized because she thinks she'll drown! Who knows whether she understands what baptism is and what it's for?" As soon as the words come out of my mouth, I want to suck them back inside. Cletus winces, and then curls his lips into his mouth. He waits for what seems like a full minute before he replies.

"NikkiMac, when I was a money-hustling drunk, you told me off, you lectured me, you even gave me money. You never wrote me off as a man doomed to stay in a broken condition. You believed God could change me into a man fit for His purpose. I know you like Angeleese and her children. Why don't you have the same vision for Angeleese as you had for me?" His voice is soft. His moist eyes question and examine me as much as his speech does. The words of the Bible that caution us to be careful with our speech come to me. I feel lower than low.

"Cletus, I'm so sorry. I let my fast tongue fly again. Out of my concern for you, I crossed the line. Will you please accept my apology?"

"Don't worry about it, NikkiMac. I still love you." Just then, the waiter brings our food. "Now, let's enjoy our meal, NikkiMac." He picks up his burger, takes a bite, chews, swallows, and grins. "Remember, lunch is on you, my sister!"

We enjoy a friendly meal. We don't say anything else about Angeleese, her children, marriage, or my big mouth.

Chapter 4

Teenager Shaylonda's Crisis

"Sister NikkiMac, can I talk with you for a minute before you and Sister Jacee leave? Just you and me, in private?" It's Shaylonda, one of the teen members of the congregation. I wonder why she's lingering after Wednesday Evening Bible class, because she's usually on the church van by now, laughing with the other teens.

Jacee nudges me before she does her famous non-whisper thing. "This certainly is a first! Miss Shaylonda usually thinks she has the answer to everything!" Of course, Shaylonda hears Jacee.

"I know you're right about that, Sister Jacee. This time, though, I think I need some help from a woman who's older than me, but not so stuffy that she'll freak out about what I have to say." The usually sassy Shaylonda wears a serious expression. She regularly attends church services, and she participates in most youth activities here. Her mother attends every now and then, but hasn't been added to the church, although she says that attending this congregation is good for her daughter.

"Of course, Shaylonda, just let me finish tidying up my classroom. You know how messy the little ones can be when we have an art project. They were supposed to paint the animals, but I think they painted everything else but the animals in Noah's ark!" Shaylonda squeezes out a smile and moves to assist me. Jacee gets the hint.

"NikkiMac, I'll call you later tonight. Okay?"

"That's cool, Jacee. Thanks for being so understanding." We had plans to meet and eat some cherry cheesecake at the newly reopened

Ewing Diner tonight. Now, the calories will have to wait a little while longer to deposit themselves on my hips.

"Shaylonda, before we begin, does your Mom know you're staying after class tonight? I don't want her to worry."

"Yes, Sister NikkiMac. I texted her that I was going to meet with you tonight and that you would drive me home afterward." It's just like Shaylonda to make plans for someone else.

"Well, next time, let me know first, Missy!" I jest, but quickly change my demeanor when I see her troubled expression. I sit in a chair and gesture for her to do the same. Shaylonda begins talking in a rapid-fire rush.

"Sister NikkiMac, I'm ashamed to tell you this and I know this is against what the Bible says but I have to tell somebody and I can't tell my mother. I like girls! I think I'm gay!" Shaylonda catches her breath and looks at me like she's about to be punished. Her eyes are as big as saucers. She searches my face, perhaps to look for signs of disapproval, judgment, or disgust.

"Baby, what makes you think you're gay because you like girls? I like women, but I'm not gay." I lean forward and give her my full attention.

"Because, Sister NikkiMac, I'm thirteen, and lots of girls my age already have boyfriends. Some of them even have sex with their boyfriends. I don't have a boyfriend and I don't want one. I don't want a boy to put his face in my face and try to kiss me on the mouth. I don't want a boy to try and hold my hand or touch my body. Boys are okay to hang out with and tease, but most of them are rude and silly. I don't have any feelings for boys! None!" She claps her hands while she delivers each syllable of the last sentence. I recognize this gesture as one of the ways that our teens add emphasis to their remarks.

"Shaylonda, I see you with the boys at church, and you seem to get along with them pretty well. You and your friend Chastity often laugh and play with these boys."

"Sister NikkiMac, they're just church boys! Who could ever get serious about them?" Shaylonda actually sounds indignant at this point, so I stifle the urge to tell her that a good church boy is probably the best type of boy to have as a male friend.

Suddenly, an uncomfortable thought forces me to begin a line of precise questioning. "Shaylonda, I want you to listen carefully. Have

21

you had any type of sexual activity with a male, with or without your consent?" I watch her face for certain revealing signs.

"No, Sister NikkiMac."

"That's good, Shaylonda. Have you had any type of sexual activity with a female, with or without your consent?" I speak softly. There's approximately two feet between our faces.

"Yes, and no, Sister NikkiMac." The teenager's expression dares me to ask exactly the right question.

"Did you kiss or touch a female in a romantic way?"

Shaylonda shivers before she replies. "There's this lady. She's younger than my mom, but older than me. She has a nice car. She's from across town. She comes to our house and does my mom's hair sometimes, and my mom pays her. This lady's always nice to me, and sometimes she brings me little treats, like candy. She always says I'm growing into a fine young lady and that she's proud of me for being a good girl. She likes that I don't let boys kiss me and do nasty things to me. The last time she came over, my mom wasn't home, but I let her in the house so she could wait. I figured it was okay because my mom knows her. I sat next to her on the sofa in the living room. At first, we mostly just talked."

"You didn't answer my question, Shaylonda. Did she touch you?" As the teenager's words start tumbling out, I feel the hairs on the back of my neck stand up.

"It was a kiss, Sister NikkiMac. I didn't start it, but I did kiss her back after she first kissed me. I liked the way it made me feel, all tingly. Her lips were very soft, and her lip gloss tasted like strawberries. My heart started beating faster and I felt hot, like it was the middle of July. Sister NikkiMac, I think I felt dizzy, and it was all because of kissing her! After a few sweet kisses, she asked me to turn on the radio and we hugged for a long time and just listened to some music she called jazz music. I remember it didn't have words, just music. About fifteen minutes before my mother came home, the lady stopped hugging me and turned off the radio. She smiled at me, took a bag of my favorite candy out of her purse, and gave it to me. She got close to my face and whispered something like this was our very first secret moment and that I should keep it between us. I agreed. Nothing else happened with her, and I haven't seen or heard from her since. That was almost a month ago, and I can't stop thinking about it. I want to do it again."

Shaylonda has a dreamy look on her face. She looks at me, but I can tell she's someplace else.

I'm disturbed, because a woman who's definitely old enough to know better is sniffing around this young teen! I mask the anger and remind myself to choose my next words carefully, because I don't want Shaylonda to clam up before I find out more about this child-molesting woman.

"Baby, is that all that happened? Did she do anything else with you? Did you tell your mother? What's this lady's name? How old is she?"

Shaylonda averts her gaze before she replies. "She's twenty-five, Sister NikkiMac, but that's not the point. Age is nothing but a number. I want to know if God will forgive me for feeling this way, for wanting this lady to be my girlfriend instead of a boy, or later on, a man. I don't want to go to hell, but I don't want to be with a boy or a man, because they can never make me feel like I felt when she kissed and held me that afternoon."

My head spins, but I attempt to stay cool. "Shaylonda, you know I'm a teacher, so you know I have to follow certain procedures in school when I find out that a child has been approached by an adult in an inappropriate way. I have the same responsibility in this situation. I have to make sure you're protected. This female you think you have romantic feelings for is older than you. She took advantage of you by kissing and holding you the way she did. She had no business asking you to keep what happened a secret between the two of you. You're not old enough to be clear on romantic or sexual feelings. You're probably still a virgin, being the active church girl that you are, right?" I hold my breath, inwardly bidding her to agree with my question.

"Yes, Sister NikkiMac, I'm still a virgin."

"Thank you, Jesus!" I whisper. "My young sister in Christ, I don't know your mother that well. In fact, I think I've only seen her a few times since you were added to the church. But this I do know: if you were my daughter and a woman had behaved like this with you, I would want to know about it. I would want to handle it. You owe your mother a chance to deal with this on your behalf."

I watch the brown eyes of the teenager moisten and fill with tears. They spill from her eyes and roll down her puffy cheeks. Her full lips quiver, and she looks so miserable and vulnerable. I have to be careful not to overreact, because this situation is personal for me. When I was a young girl, an adult male took advantage of me in a similar way. He didn't kiss me, but he did touch me inappropriately. The experience left me permanently sensitized to a child being taken advantage of in order to satisfy some twisted adult. I'm ready to lead the hunt for this woman, but I speak softly.

"Shaylonda, you're upset and confused. Trust me on this one: you're not gay. I don't think you actually know what it means to be gay. What you are is inexperienced and innocent, just the way a young Christian girl should be. I'm begging you to let me stand with you tonight while you tell your mom what happened." She appears slightly hopeful. I pray silently to God that Shaylonda will be receptive to my request. I count off ten seconds in my head while I wait for her reply.

"Okay, Sister NikkiMac. I guess I am kind of mixed up about this sex and boys and gay stuff, but I know I felt something different and good inside my body that day. I do need to tell my mom, and I want you to be there when I do."

"Thank you for telling me about this, Shaylonda. It's going to be all right. Now, let's pray to God about it, and then I'll take you home so you can tell your mom. I'll be right beside you." We both bow our heads and I say a prayer for Shaylonda before she calls her mother.

"Mom, this is Shay. I'm on my way home now with Sister NikkiMac. She says I have to tell you something that I just told her. Yes, I'm okay. I just want Sister NikkiMac to be with me while I say what I have to say. Okay, Mom, I'll see you in a little bit." The two of us leave the church building and get into my car. When we stop at a traffic light, Shaylonda turns to face me. "I'm nervous, Sister NikkiMac."

"Shaylonda, you didn't do anything wrong. Just tell your mother what you told me. I'm here for you, but more importantly, God is here. You're one of His children, and He won't leave you. That's one of the promises of God we study about in our Bible classes, right?"

"Right, Sister NikkiMac."

A few minutes later, we walk inside Shaylonda's home and face her mother. Shaylonda gives her mother a tight hug. I realize I don't know this woman's first name, so I smile and reach out for a handshake. She accepts the gesture.

"Hello, NikkiMac. I'm Iris. Thanks for bringing Shaylonda home. May I offer you something to drink? I just brewed a fresh pot of tea. It's decaf."

"Thanks, but not right now, Iris. Shaylonda's anxious, and it's probably best for her to tell you what's on her mind."

Iris holds her daughter's hands. "Talk to me, Shay. You know I love you." Shaylonda first takes a deep breath and then tells her mother the same things she told me earlier. When Shaylonda stops talking, Iris embraces her child and kisses her forehead with tenderness that brings water to my eyes. I listen as she softly whispers to Shaylonda, "Baby, you did nothing wrong. I just wish you'd told me sooner. That way, you wouldn't have carried this on your shoulders alone. Shay, how many times have I told you that I'll listen to *anything* you have to say? Even if it's something I may not like, you can still tell me. I need to know the things you're dealing with."

Shaylonda remains enveloped in her mother's arms and, for a few minutes, the teenager bawls like a toddler. Iris rubs Shaylonda's back and strokes her hair in a comforting manner. Quietly, I watch and wait. A few more minutes pass, and Iris speaks. "Shay, I want you to go into my bedroom and stretch out on my bed. Try to take a little nap. I want to speak with NikkiMac for a minute and thank her for helping you with this problem. She encouraged you to bring the matter to me, and I'm thankful to her for that. Don't you worry about a thing, because Mommy's going to handle this."

Shaylonda disengages from her mother, gives me a quick hug and a soft, "Thanks, Sister NikkiMac." She goes into her mother's bedroom. Iris turns to me, and there's fire in this mother's eyes.

"NikkiMac, that woman has done harm to my Shay, and she's got to be handled. I feel like going right up to her and putting my foot where the sun don't shine! How dare she touch my child, or anyone else's child, for that matter? She must have called herself grooming my Shay for the next level of seduction, until she got Shay to give her what she really wanted from her. As hard as I try to keep my Shay in wholesome activities and church, and this grown heifer comes after her to seduce her? No, forget about being a lady, I'm going to beat that witch down! NikkiMac, stay here with Shay. I'll be right back." Iris snatches her purse from the chair and starts for the front door.

I step in front of her. "Iris, I know you're upset, and so am I, but you don't need to confront this woman right now. What if you hurt this woman, or even kill her? That would cause even more problems for you and Shaylonda. What will happen to your daughter if you get locked up?"

"NikkiMac, I know you're a church woman and all that, but am I supposed to let this woman get away with coming to my house and petting and kissing on my child? I don't think so!"

"Wait a minute, Iris. I have an idea. One of the church members is on the police force. Let me give you his cell phone number." While I frantically search for Brother Sampson's number in my cell phone contacts list, Iris eyes me warily and paces back and forth. I find the number. "Here it is! His name is Officer Sampson, and he knows Shaylonda from church. I have faith that he'll help us handle this matter correctly. He knows the law and he knows who to talk to. This woman won't get away with taking advantage of Shaylonda, and perhaps other children will be protected. In fact, I'll call him right now. Hold on, Iris. Look, I'm dialing! Hello, Brother Sampson? This is Sister NikkiMac."

Iris stops her pacing. She listens as I quickly tell Brother Sampson what's going on and ask if he can come to Iris and Shaylonda's home. I hang up and turn to Iris. "Officer Sampson says he'll be right over."

"Thanks, NikkiMac."

"You're welcome, Iris. If you don't mind, I'll take that cup of tea now. It'll be nice to sip on while we wait for Officer Sampson."

Chapter 5

Tasha Pace Knows How To Deface

"Who's that leaning on my car?" I whisper these words as I leave the church building and head to the parking lot. The individual next to my car looks like a woman, but the person has on a hoodie, so I can't make out the face. I notice the person's hand move across my driver's side front corner panel. I shout, "Hello, can I help you?" There's no answer from the person. It's dark outside, and I should've waited for one of the brothers to walk me to my car, but I'm in a hurry to get home after Wednesday Evening Bible Class. My favorite Show, *Criminal Minds*, airs at 9 pm, and it's a new episode.

The person turns to face me. "What's up, NikkiMac? Why don't you let me hold a dollar?" It's stank Tasha Pace, the crack head daughter of my beloved Brother Foster Pace. I often wonder how such a faithful man got stuck with a bum of a child like Tasha. It's only with the Holy Spirit's help that I try to be civil to her and ignore her verbal jabs at me. A few weeks ago, her father told me that she skipped town. I certainly didn't miss her. I'm definitely not in the mood for her nonsense tonight.

"Tasha, I thought you had left town. What are you doing here, and why are you on my car? You know you have no business in this church parking lot!"

"You ask a lotta questions for somebody who ain't gave me no money yet. Anyway, I just got back to Trenton and I walked all the way down North Clinton Avenue from the train station, NikkiMac. I'm waiting for my father to come out of the building, because I need him to do me a favor."

"He's talking to some people inside, but I'm sure he doesn't want you around here." I tuck the four fingers of each hand inside my palms and make two fists.

"Why don't you let him decide that, Missy? How many times do I have to remind you that his real daughter's name is Tasha Pace, not NikkiMac? I'm his daughter, and no matter how much you drag your fat behind to church, that fact won't change!"

"Just go away, Tasha, and maybe I'll pray for you." My fingernails begin to dig into my palms.

"NikkiMac, don't tell me what to do, with your snooty self. You ain't nothin' but a phony, and this is what I think about your Christianity." Tasha hawks up phlegm. I watch her move it around in her mouth before she launches it with her rolled tongue. Her spit sails through the air and lands on my designer shoes. Her eyes glitter with craziness as she wipes her wet mouth with the back of one hand.

"Tasha, have you lost the little bit that was left of your mind?" I shout and move closer to her, but catch myself before I slap the taste out of her nasty mouth. My reaction makes her jump to the side a little, away from my car. When she moves, I see a five-letter curse word that starts with a "B" scratched into my car's paint job. Tasha keyed my car!

"That's it, Tasha! You just tore your tail with me!" My head pounds with rage and my eyes see red colors. I visualize myself grabbing Tasha by the hair, throwing her down, and pounding her head repeatedly into the pavement. Then, I realize I'm about to lose it. A small voice inside my head tells me to stop, walk away, pray, call Poppa Pace or the police, and handle this like a child of God. Instead of listening to that voice, I snatch Tasha by her collar. My intent is to force her to lick her spit off my shoes before I sit on her and call the police to report the damage to my car. Her expression is eerily defiant, with her wild, unevenly placed eyes.

Suddenly, we hear the sound of running feet. "Hey, Tasha! I know that's you! I knew your raggedy tail was coming back to Trenton before too long! Where my money at?" Two large men dressed in dark clothing approach us in the parking lot. The bigger man has a large bat. Tasha's eyes pop and her jaw goes slack. Her bravado leaves, and she looks afraid. Now, I'm scared. I take my hands off her collar.

"Mystery, Six-X, let me tell you what happened!" Tasha pleads.

"Naw, Tasha. Let me tell *you* what went down. You accepted a package from me. You was supposed to drop it off across town. Instead, you skipped town. Now, you back here in Trenton without my package and without my money. You know what's up, Tasha. Just come on and walk away with us." Mystery sounds like what he'll do to Tasha is no mystery.

Tasha grabs my arm. "Fellas, I was just leaving with my sister here. You don't want to cause no commotion in this church parking lot. You know I'll get you your money, Mystery."

I push Tasha's arm away. "Get off me, Tasha. Go on with your friends." I'm anxious, but I'm also pissed off about her spit on my shoes and her artwork in my car's paint.

Mystery looks at me with cold eyes, "Miss, this ain't got nothin' to do with you, so you can go. Our business is with Tasha." He doesn't have to tell me twice. Wordlessly, I get into my car and watch the two men take Tasha out of the dark parking lot. Each man has one of her arms. Her feet drag in useless resistance. I hear her holler out to me.

"NikkiMac, go in the church building and get my dad!" She sounds desperate, but the compassion switch in my heart is in the *off* position. I don't go back inside the church building to tell Brother Pace or anyone else. I sit in my car and watch them take her down North Clinton Avenue until I can't see them any more. Then, I drive home to watch my favorite television program. I try to make Tasha Pace the furthest thing from my mind.

Before I go to bed, my phone rings. Since the caller ID reveals it's my Poppa Pace, I answer, because I always take his phone calls. Suddenly, I think of Tasha, and I become anxious.

"Hello, Poppa Pace. What's up?"

"Daughter NikkiMac, it's about Tasha. She's in the hospital, and she's hurt really bad. I think somebody attacked her and left her for dead. The strange thing is she keeps trying to say your name. That's all I can get out of her. Do you know why she keeps mentioning you? Did you see her earlier tonight?"

At that moment, the events of the evening replay in my mind's eye like a bad movie. I visualize my car with Tasha Pace standing by it. I hear her funky words. Her spit sails through the air and lands on my shoes. A nasty word is scratched into my car's paint job. My hands snatch Tasha by her collar. Mystery and Six-X confront Tasha with words and then carry her away. I hear Tasha call me by name and ask me to get her father, my Poppa Pace.

Finally, I feel remorse. I tell Tasha's father what happened earlier this evening. After I do that, Poppa Pace tells me about my sinful behavior and then he hangs up the phone.

Chapter 6

NikkiMac's Confession

Jacee and I arrive at church on Sunday morning, and Brother Carlos greets us as we enter the lobby. "Sisters, did you hear what happened to Brother Pace's daughter, Tasha? She got a bad beatdown on Wednesday night. Somebody almost killed her!"

I try to avoid direct eye contact with Jacee and Brother Carlos. "What are you talking about, Carlos?" I hate myself for this feigned astonishment. I knew Mystery and Six-X were going to punish Tasha in some kind of way. In addition to that, I still sting from the rebuke Brother Pace delivered to me over the phone on Wednesday night.

Jacee asks, "Brother Carlos, where's Tasha?"

"At St. Francis Hospital. I think Tasha is being moved from ICU to a regular room today. NikkiMac, somebody broke her jaw. The doctors had to wire it shut. She has to take liquid food through a straw. I heard that two dudes beat her with a bat and with their fists, and one of her legs is broken, too. I know Tasha's a pain, especially to you, NikkiMac, but that doesn't give anyone the right to beat her almost to death. I wonder why they did that to her. Maybe she stole something." Brother Carlos' usual playful demeanor is absent.

Jacee sighs. "Well, I feel bad for Tasha, but a lot of bad things happen to people who roam the streets all night. I pray she'll recover and come back to church. I hope she stops trying to antagonize you, NikkiMac. At least you've gotten to the point where you can ignore her foolishness."

Our conversation in the lobby causes us to be late for the start of service. By the time we enter the auditorium, it's time for prayer

31

requests. I feel lowdown, because I didn't tell my best friend about my encounter with Tasha and the two scary men. I didn't tell Jacee that I knew Tasha was in trouble on Wednesday night. I didn't reveal to my best friend that on Thursday, I paid one of the neighborhood auto body guys to quickly fix my car's paint. On Friday, I took my spit-stained designer shoes to the downtown shoe repair shop so they could be cleaned and polished. I kept all this from her. At this moment, it's hard for me to look at Jacee's trusting face, but I realize I have to say something.

"Jacee, I owe you an explanation. Please forgive me for not telling you about this sooner, but I have to make this right with God, and some other people, too. I know I have to stand and confess my sinful behavior."

"What are you talking about? Are you getting ready to stand up, NikkiMac?" Jacee gently taps me on my shoulder, like she's comforting someone who's lost her mind.

Brother Flowers asks, "Are there any prayer requests at this time?" As I rise from my seat, I feel like I'm in a bad slow motion dream.

"Church, I've sinned. Someone did wrong to me, and in turn, I let something bad happen to that person. I didn't hurt that person physically, but in my anger, I committed sin. If I had alerted someone, the person might have received help and escaped harm. I confess my sin and I repent. I ask for forgiveness and I need prayer." My heart beats quickly, and my freckled face is red with embarrassment. I pause and listen to the whisperers.

"Is that Sister NikkiMac? What's she confessing about?"

"Who got hurt? What happened?"

I find the courage to keep speaking. "Brothers and sisters, you may have heard about Tasha Pace getting hurt. I didn't hurt Tasha, but I knew she was in trouble on Wednesday night, and I didn't tell anyone. I didn't tell because I was angry that she had keyed my car and spat on my shoes." I hear more comments.

"What!"

"Oh, my Lord!"

"That's just nasty!"

It's hard to believe that I'm at this place in my life, especially after growing so much in Christ. The Bible tells us to keep our eyes on

Christ, because if we don't, we'll walk into sin. I take a deep breath and continue.

"I offer a public apology to Brother Foster Pace, because I should have alerted him about this incident right away." Brother Pace watches me intently, but I can't read in his face if there's forgiveness for me in his heart. More whispers.

"That's right; Brother Pace does have a crack head daughter! I think I did hear she got beat up!"

"I thought she moved out of town!"

"She needs to get her trifling self in rehab and back in the church! It's a shame before the Lord, the way she carries on!"

"I offer a public apology to my sister and best friend, Sister Jacee. I didn't admit this to her before today, so she had no knowledge of this." Jacee eyes me like I just sprouted a head full of snakes.

"I offer an apology to the church because I didn't act like a Christian. I knew what to do to bring assistance, and I refused to do it. I also plan to go to the hospital after service today to offer an apology to Tasha. I've asked God for His forgiveness, and I ask for your forgiveness, because I made the church look bad." There's silence as I sit down.

Jacee quickly recovers, reaches for me, and hugs me hard. "I forgive you, NikkiMac. How could I not?" My tears are hot on my face. I hear some of the church members' reactions.

"Amen!"

"God bless you, sister!"

"Praise the Lord!"

The next touch I feel is on my shoulder. It's my Poppa Pace. "I forgive you, Daughter NikkiMac. I know I said what I had to say when you admitted what happened, but that doesn't mean I don't love you anymore or that I can't forgive." He sits down next to me and when Jacee lets me go, he hugs me. His forgiving spirit humbles me.

Brother Flowers announces, "The Bible tells us in Second Corinthians chapter 7, verse 10 that Godly sorrow leads to repentance, and that we all have sinned, according to Romans chapter 3, verse 23. Will you pray with me, church? Let's bow our heads."

At first, I find it difficult to focus on the words of Brother Flowers. My mind is on the wrong I did. I guess I got cocky, and thought I was *Super Christian*. That's why I messed up and let Tasha Pace get attacked. As I listen to the words of the prayer, my heart aches because of my awful behavior. Yet, I have a growing sense of peace because I came clean about what I did. I have a sense of hope, because I know that with God's help, I'll do better the next time I'm faced with this type of temptation. Jacee holds my hand throughout the prayer.

We sing *Praise Him! Praise Him!* as we continue our worship service. Scripture is read before we have communion. We sing *Sweet By And By* and *My Faith Looks Up to Thee.* Then, Brother Johnson preaches today's sermon. As I participate in the remainder of the worship service, the spirit of forgiveness surrounds me and I thank God for His grace.

Later on, silly Brother Carlos asks, "Sister NikkiMac, earlier, you let me rattle on and on about Tasha's beatdown, but you didn't tell me you already knew about it! Why didn't you offer me a public apology also?" He winks to let me know he's only messing with me.

I grin before I reply, "Hush up, Brother Carlos! I think I've done enough confessing for one Sunday."

He chuckles gently and says, "I heard *that*!"

After service is over, a few Christians approach me and offer their support concerning my repentance and confession. This is helpful to me. In the parking lot, Jacee asks, "Do you want to come to my parents' house for a home cooked Sunday meal? You know my folks are always happy to see you, NikkiMac."

"I'd love to, Jacee, but I'm going to the hospital to apologize to Tasha Pace. I already told her father I was going to, and he said it was probably best to handle it sooner rather than later."

"Will you be okay? Do you want me to come with you?" I note the concern in Jacee's eyes.

"Thanks, Jacee. I love you for asking, but I was the one who left her hanging and let her get beat up, not you. I need to do this alone."

"Well, at least she won't be able to say anything nasty to you if she doesn't accept your apology. Since her jaw is wired, she can't speak!" Jacee smiles broadly.

"Girl, that is so wrong. It's kind of funny, but it's wrong!" I wave goodbye to Jacee, get in my car, and head in the direction of St. Francis Hospital. There's not much traffic on North Clinton Avenue this Sunday afternoon, which is unusual. We always warn folks about trying to cross this street because it's long and winding with parking on both sides of the street, and most vehicles speed all along here. Some stretches of North Clinton Avenue have businesses, but mostly there are row homes. Drivers have to be alert for playful children who dart into the street. Other challenges for drivers are the folks who slowly cross the street while looking defiantly at oncoming vehicles. Their faces and body language say, "Hit me if you want to. I dare you, because I'll sue you!" I turn left onto Lincoln Avenue and as I approach the Lincoln Avenue Bridge, I notice the abandoned Miller Homes. This is a mostly high-rise project that was touted years ago as a model of low-income urban housing. Crime eventually got so bad there that the project was closed down. Housing lots of people in apartments in tall buildings with two elevators and little outside space doesn't work without first changing the minds of some of the people. Many people have to be taught how to live in a shared space.

Once over the bridge, I drive on Chambers Street. On the left is the old Food Fair, where my mother used to do her grocery shopping when I was a little girl. On the right is the old Fantasy Lounge, where jazz greats used to perform. This strip has changed so much since I was in high school. Speaking of high school, the front façade of Trenton High School stands majestic. The school covers the entire square block. Across the street is St. Francis Hospital. I park in the lot and mentally prepare for what I have to do.

Inside, I sign in at the visitors' desk and learn that Tasha has been moved to a room. I make my way there. At the doorway of her room, I almost lose my resolve, until I softly scold myself and pray. "Cut it out, NikkiMac. Do what you came here to do. Heavenly Father, please give me the grace to offer a sincere apology. Please help Tasha get better. In Jesus' name I pray. Amen."

I enter the room and see that Tasha is alone and appears to be asleep. She looks like a raggedy doll in the hospital bed. She wears a headscarf, which mercifully covers most of her steel wooly hair. Her face is puffy, and she has some type of apparatus around her jaw. She has blackened eyes. Her right leg is in traction. Suddenly, her eyes open and focus on me. Recognition changes to accusation.

"Hello, Tasha. I just wanted to come by and check on you." My voice sounds small. She grunts and stares at me. Then, she points to her mouth and gestures that she can't speak. Although she looks at me like I'm a waste of her time, I have to do this.

"Tasha, I know your jaw is wired shut, and that you're uncomfortable, so I won't stay long. I made a confession at church today about not getting help for you on Wednesday night when those guys grabbed you. I'm here to apologize. Tasha, I'm so sorry. I hope you'll accept my apology. What do you want me to do? Do you want me to go to the police and give them a description of those guys so they can be arrested?"

Up until I speak that last sentence, Tasha's facial expression is flat, but then she comes alive. Her head moves from side to side in what I guess a "NO!" response. "Tasha, don't you want them to be punished? I'm not afraid to tell on them. I want to make up for what I let happen to you."

She widens her uneven eyes and carefully reaches for the pad and pencil on the tray near her. There's a scratching sound as she writes. Then, Tasha hands me the notepad. The message: *Don't snitch and make more trouble for me! My problem, not yours! You're forgiven, but still not liked! Now GO!*

I silently read the note twice, tear it off the pad, and wave goodbye to Tasha. She closes her eyes and keeps them shut, as if she actually wants me to disappear. I leave her room.

Chapter 7

Church Folks Behaving Badly

I'm in the lobby before the start of Sunday worship service when I see Usher Gray frown at another member of the congregation. The person must have yawned out loud or committed some other violation that didn't meet Usher Gray's standard of approval. For some reason only he may understand, Usher Gray is crankier than usual today. He snaps at Brother Tobert, who stands in the doorway while he greets another member. I'm not the only person who notices this, because there are other expressions of disapproval. Usher Gray hisses at Brother Tobert, "Man, can't you see you're blocking the doorway? People need to pass by! Move out of the way if you want to have a conversation!" Usher Gray delivers this command with a surly look. Brother Tobert first looks startled, then indignant.

"Who do you think you're talking to in that tone of voice, Usher Gray? I'm sorry for blocking the doorway, but all you had to do was bring it to my attention, and I would have moved." Brother Tobert apologizes to the people who are about to enter.

"It's no problem, Brother Tobert. We were just about to ask you to excuse us so we could pass by you, but Usher Gray jumped in first." All of the people nearby eye Usher Gray. He notices this, and quickly shifts gears.

"Look, brothers and sisters, I'm just doing my job. I'm trying to make sure things are done decently and in order around here, like the Bible says." His voice is much softer now. Then, he notices me. "Sister NikkiMac, may I help you? Do you need something?" His fake niceness doesn't hide the fact that he can't stand me. I think it's because he knows I see through him. I'm still working on loving him with the agape that God requires, but I take issue with the way he parades himself around here like he's the church police.

"Actually, I do need something, Usher Gray. I need for you to be a lot more like Jesus when you interact with folks. That's what I need. If you can't do that, I need for the leadership here to drop you from the Ushers Committee. Got anything else you want to hear from me?" He snorts, and walks away.

Behind me, Sister Melody chimes in. "You tell him, Sister NikkiMac! He certainly does need to sit his rude self down. One time I even saw Usher Gray try to get Brother Elton to move his seat, not because a visitor needed a place to sit, but because Usher Gray wanted ten people on a pew, and Brother Elton was the eleventh person!" Of course, since this comes from Sister Melody, I can't take it to the bank. That woman knows she can exaggerate, but she's my sister in Christ. However, I haven't gotten to the point where I want to hang out with her. The interaction I have with Sister Melody at church services is the best I can do for now.

I walk to my seat and Jacee arrives a minute later. We greet each other quickly before service opens with greetings, prayer, acknowledgement of visitors, and requests for prayer by Brother Flowers.

Sister Preston stands. "I ask you all to pray for my daughter Colette. She was baptized in this church many years ago, but she stopped coming to church and got caught up out there in the streets. Now, she's in jail for assault, and I can't afford to post bail for her. Please pray that she'll allow God to help her get back on the right track."

A middle-aged sister stands. I can't remember her name, but she always smiles when she sees me. "Brother Flowers, I have a prayer request. I have a job interview tomorrow. Please pray that I'll get this job, if it's the Lord's will. Since the last company I worked for downsized and let me go, I haven't been able to find a full time job with benefits. I believe God is still looking out for me, though, because He's blessed me by keeping a roof over my head and some food on the table for my son and me. I know plenty more people are worse off than me, and I pray for them and try to help them as much as I can. I ask for prayer and I praise the Lord at the same time."

"Yes, Lord."

"Amen."

Brother Flowers offers prayer, and then the song leader starts *Holy, Holy, Holy*. Voices rise in four-part harmony as we sing praises to God. *Love Lifted Me* and *Heavenly Sunlight* are the next two hymns we sing before Brother Adam Greene comes forward to lead the scripture reading. I turn to Hebrews chapter 13, verses 20 through 21, and follow along as Brother Adam reads the verses out loud. It's hard to concentrate, because Brother Adam can be a worship distraction for me. It's not because he tries to be, it's my fault. Brother Adam is friendly to everyone, and when he's around, many single sisters as well as women visitors take notice. That man is fine. It's not my way to be so impressed with a man who hasn't shown a special interest toward me, but Brother Adam is exceptional in faithfulness as well as appearance. I lightly smack my hand, a trick I use to regain my focus. I note that the scripture reading is about how Jesus Christ will give the faithful everything needed to do His will, and that Christ will help the faithful with obedience. We stand for prayer after the Bible reading, and Brother Sanders launches into one of the long-winded prayers he's known to pray. By the time he finishes, my shoes are off and I'm sure the people with bad legs or bad feet have already returned to their seats. Five brothers come forward to lead us in communion. After communion, Brother Vonner leads *There's A Crown For Your Cross*. I smile as I sing the words of the third verse because they tell of the Savior in heaven watching and waiting for the faithful. When the song ends, Brother Johnson comes to the podium to deliver the sermon.

"Good Sunday morning to all! I appreciate the brothers who have led in the order of service thus far. I especially thank Brother Adam Greene, who must have been in my head when he selected Hebrews chapter 13, verses 20 through 21 for today's scripture reading. He probably didn't know it, but that's part of my sermon. You didn't look at my notes, did you, Brother Adam?" He smiles at the brother.

"No, Brother Johnson. I sure didn't. Not today, at least." Brother Adam chuckles, and we all laugh.

Brother Johnson continues. "God is working in me what pleases Him. God is working in you what pleases Him. I find that exciting and encouraging. I hope we all find that exciting and encouraging."

"Amen!"

"Preach, brother!"

"There's a parallel message to Hebrews chapter 13, verses 20 through 21 in Philippians chapter 2, verse 13. When we quit doing things our way and instead yield to God's will for us, He'll work in us. We can't get a better deal than that. First, God tells us what to do in the scriptures. Then, He actually helps us to live the way He wants us to live. All we have to do is get out of our own way and lean on God. By faith, He works in His obedient children. God is not a big policeman in the sky who *makes* us do what He wants. When we listen to Him, there's no room for doubt that He will help us. The question is if we'll let ourselves be available for our part in this wonderful sanctification process."

"Yes, Brother Johnson!"

"Amen!"

I hear a faint buzzing sound and notice a young lady named Carrietta Twyce twitch. Her ever-present cell phone must be in vibrate mode. She pulls the phone out of her back jeans pocket and leans forward to answer it. Then, with her cell phone cupped to her ear, Carrietta gets up from her seat on the second pew and walks quickly up the middle aisle. Her expression shows that this phone call is extremely important to her. The shoulders on her small frame hunch up, and her usual smile hides behind pursed lips. She still has some cuteness left in her chocolate drop face, but her lifestyle is quickly claiming that. When she reaches the doors, Carrietta pushes them open with such force that one of the double doors almost connects with an usher's head. Someone mutters, "I don't believe that woman is taking a phone call in the middle of the sermon!"

I shake my head. People who have attended our congregation for a while are used to Carrietta's behavior, even if they don't approve of it. Although she's never been baptized, she periodically attends worship services. She drops out of sight for months at a time, and then she comes back and tells the sordid tales of her life in the streets. She confesses and asks for prayer. After about a month, she drops out again. I don't know what's wrong with her, but the church always prays for her. Poppa Pace often reminds me that God loves Carrietta, too. After about ten minutes, Carrietta returns and marches back to her seat. Now, she has a cellophane pack of those really orange-colored cheese and peanut butter crackers and a takeout paper cup with a straw in the lid. I refuse to look at Jacee or crazy Brother Carlos, because I know what their faces are doing. However, I often wonder why the ushers don't do something about Carrietta's church violations. Maybe they aren't comfortable addressing her type of behavior. I guess some people just have to be seen, but I don't come here for the *Carrietta Show*.

Brother Vonner's voice breaks into my thoughts as he leads *Softly And Tenderly*, the song of invitation. We stand and sing all four verses. After that, four of the ushers collect the offering and then a brother starts reading the church announcements. I notice Usher Gray pick up his Bible and his coat. I guess he has to leave a little early today. As usual, the announcements go on and on, and I tune them out. All of a sudden, a loud noise from outside interrupts us.

"Screech!"

"Bang!"

Poppa Pace, Brother Adam, and Brother Carlos rush out of the auditorium. Nosy Sister Melody gets up from her seat and follows them. Soon, she's back inside and next to Jacee and me. She speaks to us with her eyes popped wide open.

"Sister NikkiMac, you won't believe this! Usher Gray took his huge truck and tried to run over Brother Tobert's little sports car with it!"

"Sister Melody, stop playing." I don't believe her, with her exaggerating self.

"I'm serious, Sister NikkiMac! Brother Tobert parked his car in one of the handicapped spaces, and Usher Gray rammed it with his truck. On purpose, I bet!"

There's a buzz in the auditorium. Brother Johnson and Brother Adam return and both men step to the pulpit. Brother Johnson speaks, "Brothers and sisters, I'm sad to say that we just saw behavior that's unbecoming for Christians. One of our brothers inappropriately parked his car in a space marked for handicapped parking. We regularly ask that you only park cars with handicapped stickers in these spaces. Usher Gray became angry when he saw a car parked there without a sticker. In his anger, he lost control and attacked the car with his truck. As your minister, I had to address both brothers' behavior with them. I did that outside, and Brother Adam Greene is my witness. Brother Adam nods. He looks solemn.

The congregation reacts. "Amen! Amen!"

Our minister continues, "Brother Tobert repented for ignoring the parking rule and he's returned to apologize to the congregation for his part in this situation. Usher Gray was not repentant nor receptive to reconciliation, so he won't be serving as an usher until further notice. He's still our brother, though, and we should all do our part to encourage his repentance and growth in Christ."

"That's right, Brother Johnson."

"Help us all, Lord Jesus!"

"Yes and indeed!"

Brother Johnson closes his eyes for a couple of seconds before he continues. "Now, let's stand on our feet, bow our heads, and go to the Lord in prayer."

Chapter 8

Assistant Minister Adam Greene

"God has blessed us with a beautiful Sunday morning. He woke us up this morning, guided us on our way to worship service, and we're here to praise Him. Isn't that right, church?"

"Amen, Brother Vincent!"

"Glory to God!"

"Let's lift up our voices in song. Join me in singing *Hallelujah! Praise Jehovah!* Brother Vincent's strong voice leads us in a rousing start to the song portion of our worship service. Our voices blend in sweet harmony. Well, most of our voices do. Sister Melody sings in her familiar loud falsetto that defies any effort to achieve full vocal harmony. I look at Jacee and we both shake our heads. Thankfully, Brother Vincent is such a capable song leader that the witchy voice of Sister Melody doesn't throw him off key. We sing two more hymns, then have communion. When Brother Vincent returns to the front, he makes a statement. "Brothers, sisters, and visiting friends, a few weeks ago, our leadership announced the appointment of Brother Adam Greene as our assistant minister. We're glad you're here today to witness his official installation. Minister Johnson?"

Brother Johnson stands before the congregation. He motions for Brother Pace and a minister from a sister congregation to join him up front. Then, he speaks to Brother Adam Greene. "Would you please join us up front?" Brother Greene does so, and the men place their right hands on Brother Greene's shoulders. "As most of you know, Brother Greene came to us a while ago from a sister congregation in Huntsville, Alabama. In the letter of recommendation from the

Huntsville church leadership, Brother Adam Greene was commended. He's been a hard worker in the church, and we're going to press him into service as our assistant minister." Brother Johnson reads passages of scripture, and Brother Adam Greene verbally accepts the responsibilities of this ministry. The ministers offer prayer for Brother Greene in his new role.

We all say, "Amen."

"Now, before anyone grumbles about Brother Greene not being a married family man, who told you that the assistant minister had to be a married man? Brother Greene is sound in his knowledge of scripture and his work here shows that he can be of further assistance to the leadership here. Besides that, I'm confident that Brother Greene is capable of changing his marital status if and when he feels he needs to do so! If you want to know more about his personal life, ask him." I hear whispers and some giggling. Then, Carrietta Twyce shouts her approval.

"Alright now, Assistant Minister Greene!"

"Calm down, Carrietta," cautions Brother Johnson. She has enough temporary sense to give a sheepish, compliant smile. "Church, please give Brother Greene your Christian support as we all go forward to make this congregation a light to the world. Let's all focus on teaching the gospel and walking in the Spirit. Amen?" Brother Johnson offers another prayer for Brother Greene and the congregation.

"Amen, Brother Johnson!"

"I know that's right!"

"After our next song selection, Brother Greene will preach this morning's sermon." Brother Johnson takes his seat.

Brother Vincent says, "Please turn to number 13 in your songbooks and join me in singing *Wonderful Words of Life*, a beautiful and encouraging hymn."

Jacee whispers to me. "Brother Greene is so fine that I wonder how he managed to stay single for this long. I know he's in his forties, probably about the same age as we are. What's up with that, NikkiMac? I know you and I have never been married, but the odds are in favor of men finding mates. What's his story?"

"Jacee, how do you know he's never been married? He might be a widower, for all we know! I don't have the answer to your question, but I'm sure you aren't the only woman in this room with the same thoughts."

"I know, NikkiMac. Sister Melody must be deliriously happy about this turn of events. She may have the chance to date an assistant minister who's also fine!" Jacee lightly elbows me in jest, but I'm not sure I like the mental picture of Sister Melody dating Brother Adam. I'm friendly to Brother Adam, but I don't chase him down, unlike several of the other church sisters do. He and I have worked on some church teaching projects, and they were productive. He was totally on task during our work time, pleasant, but focused. I find him attractive, but one would have to be sightless to think otherwise. The man is a real eyeball massage, but there's more to his appeal. He's extremely focused on the Bible and on working for the good of the church. His attitude and his character are just as attractive as his looks. Besides, I'm in a place right now where I'm not actively chasing romance. If it's to be, it'll come.

The song ends and Brother Adam Greene speaks. "I thank God for the opportunity to stand before you to proclaim the gospel. I appreciate the confidence that Brother Johnson and the rest of the church leaders have in me. By God's grace, I'll serve you the best I can as your brother and assistant minister. Please keep me in prayer. At this time, I want to draw your attention to the word of God. I'm here to tell you that God is working in us according to His good pleasure. If you're taking notes, and to help out the brothers who are doing the tape and CD ministry, let's use that statement as a title for this message, *According to God's Good Pleasure*. It's taken from Hebrews chapter 13, verses 1 through 21, with the focus on verses 20 and 21. In chapter 13, as the writer concludes the book of Hebrews, he deals with rules for living the Christian life. In verses 20 and 21, the speaker asks for a blessing on the hearers, and he tells them that God is a God of peace. Remember, our divine Father is not the God of confusion. Therefore, we should not be people of confusion. We read here that through Jesus Christ, God works in us what pleases Him. He knows what He wants us to be, and He works it out in us, if we allow Him to do so. Are we living by our will, or living according to the will of God? In faith, there's only one right way to live." Brother Greene pauses and looks over the audience.

"Preach it!"

"Amen! Amen!"

Brother Greene continues, "Aim to please God. Some people make it complicated, but it's not. God is pleased when we love His Son. God is pleased when we love and obey Him. His commands show us what pleases Him, and the commands are found in the Bible."

"That's right!"

"Say so, preacher!"

"God's will is an internal matter. It's of the heart, the whole of the inner person, the human spirit. Let your life testify that the Holy Spirit works in you!" Brother Greene preaches for a few minutes more, then we stand for the invitation song, *I Am Praying For You*. After that, the brothers collect today's offering, and Brother Martin reads the announcements.

"In two weeks, we'll have our monthly Sunday Fellowship meal. The Kitchen Committee will prepare all the meats, but we're asking members to bring vegetables and side dishes. There's a signup sheet for this in the lobby, but no one has signed up to bring any of these items. Come on, folks! I know some of you are experts at fixing collard greens, black-eyed peas, string beans, dirty rice, potato salads, macaroni salads, and all kinds of other veggie and side dishes. Please go out to the lobby after dismissal and write the name of your specialty dish on the signup sheet." Just then, little Sasha Coles darts down the center aisle and laughs gleefully as she swings her raggedy stuffed teddy bear. As is her pattern, she's escaped from her parents, Brother and Sister Coles. The chubby toddler almost reaches Brother Martin before her father catches her. She squeals with joy. Sasha likes this game.

"Okay, little Sasha, I see you're ready to move. I only have a few announcements today!" Brother Martin smiles at the little one. "All ladies who want to participate in the Secret Sisters activity should meet with Sister Sharlette Johnson, our minister's wife, in the conference room right after service today." I zone out for the next few minutes, because like Sasha, I have a hard time paying attention during the announcements. Unlike Sasha, I don't have the liberty of running down the aisle while they're being read. After the closing prayer, Jacee and I greet members in the auditorium before we head for the lobby, where Brother Johnson and Brother Greene wait to shake hands with church members and visitors.

"Good sermon, Brother Greene. I'm glad to have you as our assistant minister." Sister Hobson sounds sincere.

"Thank you, my sister." Brother Greene replies in a soft voice. While Brother Flowers greets the ministers and Jacee, I try to scoot past. However, Jacee puts me on blast.

"NikkiMac, don't you want to congratulate Brother Greene?" I give her a dirty look, which she ignores. As my face burns with embarrassment, I'm sure my cheeks are red and my freckles are popping. Why's Jacee showing out like this?

Brother Johnson reaches out and shakes my hand. "Hello, Sister NikkiMac. It's good to see you today."

"Hello, Brother Johnson. It's good to see you, too." With my peripheral vision, I notice the gaze of Brother Adam Greene. Then, I hear his voice. It sounds more animated than shy.

"Hello, Sister NikkiMac. I'm happy to see you. You know, I've been meaning to ask you something. Would you mind giving me your phone number?" He holds my hand a few seconds longer than Brother Johnson did when he greeted me. Brother Greene's attractive smile captivates me.

"My ph-ph-phone number?" When did I develop a stutter?

"Yes, my sister. With your permission, I'd like to call and ask you a question in private. It's personal." I think I detect a twinkle in his eye. Brother Johnson beams at the two of us. I wonder if he knows something I don't know.

Jacee exclaims, "My, my, my!"

Sister Melody, who thinks all the single men in the congregation should want the pleasure of her attention, joins Brother Adam Greene and me and creases her brow. Jacee quickly moves Sister Melody a polite distance away and engages her in conversation. I take a business card from my purse and hand it to our new assistant minister. "Here's my card, Brother Greene. You have permission to call me, my brother." I smile and try to steady my knocking knees before I walk away to join Jacee and Sister Melody. I can hardly wait to get home so I can do my happy dance.

Chapter 9

The Sisters Meet

Today, many women of the church gather in a meeting room. Sister Sharlette Johnson, our minister's wife, stands before the group of chattering sisters. Instead of asking for everyone's attention, Sister Sharlette begins singing *My Faith Looks Up to Thee*. Her lovely soprano voice draws the attention of the ladies. Conversation stops, and we join her in song. It's nice to hear all women's voices; there's an angelic sweetness in the sound. At the end of the song, we all say, "Amen!"

"Sisters, I asked you to meet with me this Sunday afternoon to help me organize Project Harmony. It's an effort to have us fellowship with each other on a more personal level. It's good for us to get to know one another more, so we can learn to care about each other more. In Acts chapter 2, verses 42 through 47, the Bible tells us about the closeness of the saints in the early church. Christians supported one another in a variety of ways. They sacrificed, when needed, to help each other. We want to avoid cliques. We don't want any sister to feel like she's alone in her Christianity. We especially want to give strong friendship to new sisters, because some of them are the only church members in their households. We know that people tend to gravitate to people with whom they have something in common, but how many of us know each other well enough to know what else, besides the faith, we have in common? By a show of hands, how many of you know the last names of all the sisters in this room?" About ten women raise their hands. There are some nervous giggles.

"Do you see what I mean? By a show of hands, how many of you know the first name of each sister in this room?" Only Sister Johnson raises her hand. "This makes my point. How can we love each other the way God wants us to if we don't know each other?"

"I don't have a problem with getting to know other sisters, but I don't want everybody all up in my business, Sister Sharlette!" It's Sister Terrie Towns. She hasn't been worshipping here that long. She came from a congregation in Philadelphia, and she's always negative and critical. My nickname for her is "Negative Terrie."

I whisper to Jacee, "She always finds a reason to complain about anything that's not her idea."

"I know that's right," Jacee replies.

Sister Sharlette remains calm. She knows the negative style of Sister Towns. "I hear what you're saying, Sister Towns. Project Harmony is not about being nosy. It's about showing care."

"Amen, Sister Sharlette!"

Sister Arpaige Baker speaks up. "I wouldn't mind getting to know more sisters, but I usually have to work on Sunday mornings. That's why I'm not as familiar with folks as I could be. I attend on Sunday evenings, but there are always fewer people here at night, so I miss interacting with several of you. I know a lot of you by face, but not by name. Sister Johnson, please tell us more about how this project will work." Sister Arpaige has a teen son who had some problems in the past, but now he's quite active in our youth program.

"Thanks for that, Sister Arpaige," says Sister Johnson. "I envision a monthly sisters gathering here, where we begin with prayer, participate in get-acquainted activities, plan goodwill projects for others, and enjoy light refreshments. It doesn't have to be more than an hour or an hour and a half each time. We could schedule it for a Saturday afternoon. I encourage participation from all the sisters in the congregation."

Sister Towns interrupts, "Sister Johnson, you can't make people come and be a part of this. This is supposed to be the church! Besides, it sounds like sorority stuff to me!"

Jacee squirms. I can tell she's about to burst. I whisper, "Wait for it, wait for it . . ."

"Sister Towns, what's wrong with us dedicating some time to hang out with each other for an hour one Saturday out of a month? It sounds like it could be fun!" Jacee is emphatic, but I can tell she's not angry.

Sister Sharlette maintains a pleasant facial expression and presses on. "Sister Towns, that's not what I'm proposing. This is about a dedicated time for us to interact, not the creation of a club. Participation is voluntary."

Negative Terrie is getting warmed up. As a result, her argument takes a different direction. "Humph! It sounds like a lot of cliques will come out of this mess! It's a shame before the Lord to cause division in the church, and I want no part of this foolishness!"

I've had enough of this, so I say, "Excuse you, Sister Towns! Could you please give Sister Sharlette a chance to further explain this project? She can't do that with you badgering her. The rest of us want to hear what she has to say. Maybe someone else has questions. Please let her continue without any more interruptions."

Sister Towns pops her eyes in my direction. "Oh, so just because she's the minister's wife, I can't ask her any questions? Is that what you're saying to me, Sister McQuaige?" It's clear she's trying to piss me off by using my last name. Everybody here addresses me as Sister NikkiMac, because they know I like it that way. I'm not about to get drawn into a fight, so I take a breath and slip into my gentlest voice.

"My dear Sister Towns, it's not like that. It's about treating our sister the way we'd like to be treated if we were trying to make a presentation before this group. Isn't that the essence of Matthew chapter 7, verse 12?"

I hear a lot of voices say, "Amen!"

"That's what the Bible says." It's Sister Lolah Maze. Her twin, Sister Lelah Maze, nods her head and grins.

The usually quiet Sister Longstreet, who ended an unhealthy relationship with Butch Mathers after she embraced the faith, speaks out. "That's the thing I love most about the church, and what helps me so much. When we treat each other the way the Bible tells us to, we have peace." There's a pause in the room after Sister Longstreet's remark.

Sister Towns gives us all the evil eye. Then, she turns to leave the room. She's eerily silent. No one tries to stop her except Sister Lovey Grace, who reaches out for Sister Towns as she walks by and says, "Please don't leave, Sister Towns."

Sister Towns draws back and replies, "Sister Lovey, you just got in the church, so you don't know. You seem like a wise older woman. You'll find out how they are!" We silently watch as Sister Towns walks away.

Sister Johnson addresses the group, "Before I continue, let it be clear that I wish Sister Towns had stayed here with us. I plan to discuss this with her privately to see if we can have a better understanding. That's one reason I want us to try Project Harmony, because I think it will help us understand each other better so we won't take disagreements personally. Even when we don't agree, we're still supposed to love each other. That's God's will for us."

"Amen, Sister Johnson!"

"I'd like to make a suggestion for our first activity. I'll pass out cards with numbers one through four. I've marked off four areas of this room with signs. All of us who have the same number will sit together in the area where that number is posted. In these groups, let's do a blessings count. Each group will assign a recorder, and at the end of the session, we'll share all the blessings listed by the groups. Let's see how many blessings we list and how many of us share common blessings. Hopefully, this activity will make us more aware of how good our God is to us." Heads turn, women whisper.

"Oh, I was wondering what those numbers were about."

"Me, too!"

"This should be fun!"

"I hope I get in a group with people who want to work. I get tired of being the hardest worker on a project," mumbles Sister Melody. The eyes of a few sisters widen and their eyebrows rise, but the sisters don't say anything. All except for elderly Sister Blake, who simply can't let Sister Melody's words go unchallenged.

"I can't believe that came out of your mouth, Sister Melody. Everybody knows you do more primping and complaining than working."

Sister Melody bristles. "Oh no, you didn't! I'm not going to say anything back to you, Sister Blake, because I was raised to respect old people."

Sister Sharlette remains calm and optimistic as she speaks, "Sisters, let's take a time out here and sing two hymns of encouragement, praise, and fellowship." She begins singing *Blest Be The Tie* and we join in with sweet harmony. We follow this hymn with *He Leadeth Me*. The air in the room becomes more positive, and we move into our groups for the activity.

Jacee remarks, "Sister Johnson has the patience of Job! When it comes to working with a bunch of women, she's my *shero*."

"What's that? You're forever making up words, Jacee."

"NikkiMac, get with the program. A *shero* is a female hero: a *she* who is a *hero*. I've got to give Sister Sharlette her props."

I leave it alone. I don't bother to remind my best friend that the word for a female hero is *heroine*.

Chapter 10

Out Of Our Seats and Into The Streets

It's early Sunday afternoon, and Minister Johnson is about to divide us into teams to start another church evangelism project. Our mission is to knock on doors, pass out religious tracts, and invite people to our congregation. I live in this East Trenton neighborhood where the church meets, but most of the church members live in other parts of Trenton or in the nearby townships of Ewing, Hamilton, or Lawrence. Some members come from towns farther away.

"Alright brothers and sisters, our morning worship service is over. Now we're going to give an hour of our time to the community. We have our feeding program to assist with physical food. We need to share spiritual food in a more direct way. We have the radio ministry, some home Bible studies, but we can do more. The church is responsible for leading souls to Christ. How does it look if we don't extend personal invitations to people in the very community where we meet?"

"That's right, brother!"

"Here are your teams of four. I've assigned at least two men per team. For reasons of safety, we don't want our sisters knocking on doors alone. God wants us to evangelize, but He also wants us to be wise. Oh, just a reminder, don't put the religious tracts in the residents' mailboxes, because we want to follow the postal service's rules. Use this special tape to attach our handouts to the doors. It'll hold but not do any damage to the paint." Brother Johnson distributes rolls of tape, literature, and team lists. When I get my list, I see that my other team members are Brother Carlos, Brother Adam Greene, and Sister Chloe.

I wonder why I got assigned to work with this cold sister. She doesn't seem to like me, and I still don't know why.

"See you later," says Jacee. "I'm on the team with Sister Longstreet, Brother Foster Pace, and Brother Vincent. We're walking on Oak Street. What street is your team walking on, NikkiMac?" She sees my list, and she knows I'm not feeling Sister Chloe. Jacee sounds lighthearted but her eyebrows knit.

"I think we're going to Dickinson Street. Isn't that right, Sister Chloe?" I figure it's good to engage her in conversation, since we'll be spending the next hour together.

Sister Chloe, who's been focused on the two brothers on our team, casts a neutral look at Jacee. Then, she looks at me, and I do think her nostrils flare like she smells something rotten.

"We are indeed assigned to Dickinson Street, Sister McQuaige. Please pay attention." Before I can open my mouth to respond to Sister Chloe, Brother Adam Greene speaks up.

"Sisters, are you ready? Brother Carlos and Sister Chloe can work one side of the street, and Sister NikkiMac and I will do the other." I wonder if Brother Adam caught the funky vibe Sister Chloe sent my way and decided to split us two women up before it could get even funkier. "Let's cross the street here and start with the houses on the far end. We'll work our way back to this street." The four of us cross the street. Some of the sidewalks are broken, and there's a mixture of old brick pieces and dirt where the intact bricks used to be long ago. We have to be careful so we don't twist our ankles. Brother Adam Greene is at my side. Brother Carlos and Sister Chloe walk on the other side of Dickinson Street. A fat alley cat crosses in front of my partner and me. It pauses to stare and twirl its tail, a signal that it doesn't automatically run from humans. We reach the first door. Brother Adam knocks. A dog barks, and I immediately step back. Although I want to invite people to church, I'm not trying to get mauled by a pit bull or any other type of dog. I don't plan to go out like that.

"What? Who is it?" A man's husky voice travels through the closed wooden door.

"Hello, we're from the church nearby. We came by to invite you to worship with us and study the Bible." Brother Adam sounds respectful and caring.

"Okay, you invited me. Now, go away." The man behind the door sounds a bit perturbed.

"Sir, I have some information about the church to give you. It's our schedule of services and a tract that tells you what the church is about."

"Just leave it on the porch, and I'll get it later." I can tell that he's walking away from the door and from us, because his voice sounds more distant.

"Alright, I'll just attach it to the door."

"Whatever, man."

We've been dismissed. I look at Brother Adam. Instead of disappointment, there's peace in his expression.

"I'm sorry the man didn't open the door and speak with us, Brother Adam."

"Oh, don't be, Sister NikkiMac. Look at it this way; he didn't curse us out. He told us to leave the written material. Who knows? The next time he opens his door, he'll see our information and maybe even read it."

As I walk to the next house with Brother Adam, I pay less attention to the barking dog sounds. This time, I ring the doorbell, and listen to my heart flutter while I wait for a response. I'm a little nervous about being rejected, but I gain strength and confidence from Brother Adam's presence. All of a sudden, the door flies wide open and Mad Maggie appears. This is the same woman who we thought was homeless, because she used to come into the church building and take birdbaths in the women's room sink. She has a house?

Mad Maggie eyes me up and down before she says, "Hey heifer! What you ringin' my doorbell for?" Then, she recognizes me. "Wait a minute! Ain't you the one who told I was washin' up in the church bathroom? You the reason the men asked me to leave the bathroom that day! How would you feel if I had done that to you? It don't matter anyhow, because as you can see, I don't need to use your church bathroom sink no more. I got a place here with Neet-Neet! How you like me *now*, heifer from the church around the corner?"

I'm speechless, so Brother Adam gently steps in front of me and takes over. He speaks pleasantly and respectfully to Mad Maggie. Whoever this Neet-Neet is, she must be as bad off as Mad Maggie or she must be a saint to let this crazy woman live with her. Interestingly,

Mad Maggie speaks with Brother Adam like she has some sense. She tells Brother Adam that her real name is Madilyn and that long ago, she worked in the factory at the end of Perrine Avenue. Then, she smiles demurely at him through her snaggle-toothed mouth and graciously accepts the church literature from him. I can hardly believe this is the same bag lady with a bad attitude who almost told me off in the church restroom a while back. Her mouth looks like a checkerboard as her smile expands for Brother Adam. I am too through, and I'm glad when we leave. As we walk away, Brother Adam doesn't say anything to me about Mad Maggie, so I keep my opinion about her to myself.

We get no answer at the next five or six houses, so we attach the invitations and tracts to the doors and keep moving. Disappointment keeps me quiet, but I'm determined to see this task through. My thoughts must show on my face, because Brother Adam remarks, "Sister NikkiMac, don't be discouraged. All we can do is the best we can. The Lord sees our efforts."

"Thanks, Brother Adam. I know you're right, that's why I'm going to take the lead at the next house, okay?" To my surprise, when I ring the doorbell of the last house on the street, a woman answers the door.

"I was watching at the window and saw you all walking the street with tracts and knocking on doors. Come in, I'll listen to what you two have to say about church."

"Thank you," I reply with gratefulness. "My name is Sister NikkiMac, and this is Brother Adam Greene, our assistant minister. He'll tell you about the church, and we won't take much of your time." On our way into the lady's house, I look across the street and see a surprised look on Sister Chloe's face. I guess she didn't think Brother Adam and I would be invited into a house on Dickinson Street today.

After we leave the lady's house with her promise that she'll attend a church service soon, I feel encouraged. The hour went by a lot faster than I thought it would. I like working with Brother Adam Greene. He has a nice way with people. We return to the church building and he walks me to my car in the parking lot. Before we part ways for the afternoon, Adam shakes my hand and remarks, "It was a pleasure to work with you, Sister NikkiMac. By the way, I haven't lost your phone number. It's just that I've been swamped with my job and church work. Please bear with me. I still have something important to ask you."

Before I can say, "Ask me right now," his cell phone rings. He answers it, and a serious expression spreads across his handsome face.

"Sister NikkiMac, please excuse me. Brother Johnson needs me to fill in for him at a home Bible study. Looks like this door-to-door evangelism is working already!" His eyes light up with excitement.

"Go, Brother Adam. I understand." He pats me on my shoulder, watches me get into my car, and then quickly walks away. I'm a little frustrated that Adam couldn't finish his conversation with me, even though I'm touched by his enthusiasm for teaching the gospel. His church work is such a high priority for him that I wonder if he has time for a personal life with me or any other woman. Is this what a preacher's wife has to deal with? Does a preacher's wife ever feel that her husband's ministry overpowers their marriage? I shake my head and then chuckle before I exclaim, "Like I'm ever going to be a preacher's wife! Don't be ridiculous, NikkiMac!"

Chapter 11

NikkiMac's Church Guest

As we finish the first verse of *Trust And Obey*, an usher approaches me. "Sister NikkiMac, there's a white lady in the lobby who says you invited her to church and she wants to sit with you." I wonder who it is. Even though I often invite friends and acquaintances to visit our congregation, no one has accepted my invitation lately.

Jacee blurts, "Why does he feel like he has to specify the race of your visitor? It's not like all the members here are black! He's such a clown!" Even though I agree with Jacee, I ignore her, because I'm trying to stay out of mouth trouble today.

"Thanks," I whisper to the usher, and I get up to follow him. As I walk up the aisle, I think of how some of the older Christians who are originally from the south hold their pointer finger up when they walk the aisle during service. I guess that means, "Excuse me for walking during service." I don't hold up my finger, but I avoid strutting and try to be as inconspicuous as possible.

Standing in the lobby and looking as beautiful as she does at the school where we both work is Anna Maria DelGrosso. She tosses her fluffy shoulder-length brunette mane of hair and smiles when she sees me. Her blue eyes remind me of the ocean. Her natural lashes look to be an inch long. "NikkiMac, here I am. You've invited me to church so many times that I decided to surprise you and visit today!"

"Anna Maria, I'm glad you're here! Welcome!" We embrace, and I lead her to the auditorium doors. One of the ushers opens them, and Anna Maria and I walk the aisle to the pew. Some heads turn, because Anna Maria is a new face, but one can't ignore her creamy complexion, gorgeous long lashes, rosy lips, and bouncy hair. She's dressed in a classy navy suit, and she wears the designer shoes with the red soles. Her two gleaming link bracelets are fine Italian 18 carat yellow gold, and her hoop earrings are also the real deal. She's about my height, 5 feet, seven inches. Whatever the medical weight chart lists for a woman of her height, I'm sure Anna Maria is within the guidelines. I don't meet those guidelines, but I'm not jealous of her. She's a looker, and she's a genuinely nice person. She's also the best school secretary in the district, if you ask me. Anna Maria knows the system and she knows the paperwork. I think she's about 35 years old. She became part of the district secretarial staff a few years after her graduation from Trenton High School, and sometime later, a secretarial school. After earning her degree, Anna Maria applied to the Trenton school system and was put under the tutelage of an aged, but efficient battle-ax secretary in the North Clinton Avenue administration building. The battle-ax was too mean to retire, but she did die. Anna Maria was in the right place at the right time, and she absorbed information like a sponge. She could have continued to work at the administration building, but she requested and got a transfer to our elementary school. I was told that she'd rather work with teachers and students than in the administration building.

The first time I met her in the school office, she asserted in a no-nonsense tone, "Ms. McQuaige, just let me know how you want your office student data organized. My objective is to make it as easy as possible for the teachers to teach. That's what it's about in a school. I'll minimize the paperwork for you teachers as much as I can so you can get more teaching done." I couldn't believe my ears, because many school secretaries act as if teachers are necessary nuisances who should not spend too much time in the rarified air of the school office. Anna Maria knows more about running an elementary school office than most school office staff, including some school principals. Lately, she and I have been eating lunch together during the workday. She's Italian American and I'm African American, but we have a lot in common as far as our upbringing. Our parents had a lot of the same rules and ethics. She grew up in a mostly Italian North Trenton neighborhood, but not many Italians live there now. Neighborhoods change.

Anna Maria and I reach our pew and sit down just as a brother begins the scripture reading. Jacee nods a greeting to Anna Maria, and I hand her a visitors' Bible so she can follow along. "What do I need a

Bible for, NikkiMac? Isn't he going to read for all of us?" Anna Maria seems puzzled.

"Yes, Anna Maria, but we read along silently in our Bibles." Jacee nods her head in agreement.

Anna Maria purses her cute lips and then responds, "I've never heard of it done that way before. We do it differently where used to worship. Okay, help me find the scripture he just announced." After the scripture reading, we stand for prayer.

Following prayer, our song leader reminds us, "The next song is *Lead Me To Calvary*. It sets the tone for showing appreciation to Jesus Christ for His supreme sacrifice for mankind." After the last verse of the hymn, five brothers stand to lead the communion.

When Brother Sanders gets to the part, "Let's bow our heads in prayer for the blessing of the bread and the fruit of the vine," a cell phone sends out a musical ring tone that describes someone's hands all over another's body. The cell phone offender at first acts like he doesn't know it's his phone.

"Oh my!" whispers Anna Maria, "How disrespectful that is to Jesus!" Her lush, dark eyebrows crinkle with disapproval. I can see that Anna Maria has a strong respect for God and Christ. Service continues with Brother Vincent leading us in the singing of *Hilltops of Glory*. Anna Maria can really sing! Her voice sails over the top of the others while it caresses the melody. I notice some members look at Anna Maria and nod their heads in appreciation of her singing.

Jacee exclaims, "Wow! Lovely!" and gets back to her almost-soprano vocals.

I ask, "Anna Maria, how do you know these songs? Do you sing them at your congregation?"

"No, but I can sight-read music, NikkiMac. I was a featured soloist in the Trenton High School choir and the special singing group. I learned a lot from Mr. Mulder, who inspired me to develop my singing voice. I studied music after high school and even did some performing. That was before I got sidetracked. But, we can talk more about that later. I want to hear this sermon."

"Okay," I reply, and turn my attention to our minister.

"Unannounced, Jesus Christ is going to step back into time." Minister Johnson takes a long pause and looks over the congregation.

Jacee attempts to whisper, "Perhaps he's giving Jesus time to let his words marinate in our minds." I gently elbow her, and she gets quiet.

"Brothers, sisters, and visiting friends, will you be ready to meet Jesus when He returns? Will He receive you with words of welcome, or will He reject you and send you to eternal punishment?" Brother Johnson waits for responses.

"Amen."

"Help me, Lord."

"Yes, Lord!"

"If you die today or tonight, are you confident that it will be well with your soul? I know many of you don't want to hear me talk about death, but death is coming. We won't live in these earthly bodies forever. I will die and you will die; the Bible tells us in Hebrews chapter 9, verse 27. We reach to God for the grace to live righteously because we want to see His face in peace on the Day of Judgment. Here's the amusing part: lots of folks say they want to be with Jesus, just not right now, because they don't want to die right now! We study this often in our Bible classes, but all of you don't come to our Bible classes, isn't that right?" Brother Johnson chastises, and then shows a broad smile.

Those who attend Bible classes agree with Brother Johnson. The people who don't attend Bible classes are mostly quiet, except for one brother who mutters, "Not that again! He preaches long enough on Sunday mornings!"

Brother Johnson continues, "I invite you to attend Bible study and Sunday school classes so we can all know God and find out what He requires of us. Please put this in your notes. The Bible tells us in First Thessalonians chapter 5, verse 23 that we consist of spirit, soul, and body. At death, our bodies begin to decay and go back to the dust. Read Genesis chapter 3, verse 19. At death, our spirits go back to God. He gave them to us for this earthly life. Read Ecclesiastes chapter 12, verse 7. Our souls will live on after death. At the judgment, the souls of those who lived in disobedience to God will go to everlasting punishment. The souls of those who lived faithfully will live joyfully and eternally in God's presence in heaven. Jesus has prepared an eternal home for the faithful. Let's look at John chapter 14, verses 2 and 3." Pages turn, and we read the scripture. "I know I've shared this with you before, but it bears repeating. Put Revelation chapters 21 and 22 in your notes. Read these chapters during your personal Bible study times and take a glimpse at the glorious eternity promised for those who do God's will."

"Say so, Preacher!"

"Praise God!"

"Brother Vincent, please lead us in a verse or two of *Where The Soul Never Dies*. As a matter of fact, let's sing the whole hymn. Those words have such agreement with our sermon today." Brother Johnson steps aside and Brother Vincent starts the song. After the song, Brother Johnson continues the sermon and we have the remainder of our morning worship service. I notice that Anna Maria pays close attention and writes notes on a small pad.

After service is over, we greet others and shake hands. Some brothers make a point of walking over so I can introduce them to Anna Maria. One of them is Darius Muse.

"Hello, Miss. Welcome to our congregation. My name is Darius Muse, and I'm happy you decided to visit with us today." He extends his right hand. He has to, because the left arm from the elbow down was amputated years ago after Darius' fight with a man. The man was a brother who didn't like the way Darius treated his sister. As a result, Darius has a prosthetic forearm and hand. The skin color of it is off, though. Darius looks innocent enough these days, but I still don't fully trust him.

"Thank you, Mr. Muse. I'm Anna Maria DelGrosso. I work with NikkiMac." Anna Maria returns his greeting with a professional handshake and a crisp reply.

"Is that so? Sister NikkiMac, I see you've been evangelizing. I admire that. I need to improve in that area." I don't know why he's attempting to make conversation with me, but I'm not feeling it. I simply nod my head to acknowledge his words. He gets my drift, and returns his attention to Anna Maria.

"I hope this won't be your last visit, Miss DelGrosso. It is Miss, isn't it?" Jacee rolls her eyes at the ceiling. Anna Maria is composed as she ignores his probe of her status.

"I plan to attend more worship services here." Her expression is polite, but the set of her jaw reveals she's had enough of this fly chat. Darius moves away.

"NikkiMac, I don't know him, but I'm getting to know you pretty well. Did Mr. Muse do something to you?"

"Maria, you're as sharp as a tack, like my father, Nickson McQuaige, used to say. I'll tell you about it later. Jacee and I are going to the diner in Ewing. Why don't you join us?"

"I'd love to! Thanks for the invitation. I'll meet you both there." Anna Maria smiles and exits the church building. I notice that Jacee watches Anna Maria leave, but she doesn't say anything. I'll have to ask Jacee about that later.

Chapter 12

Cletus and Angeleese

It's early Saturday evening, and following a song and praise gathering, a few church members stand around in the church parking lot. Jacee and Brother Carlos help Poppa Pace get a couple of elderly sisters into the church van. Cletus walks over to me.

"NikkiMac, I've made up my mind. I've prayed on it and turned it over and over in my head. I'm getting tested to see if those twins are my babies." Cletus looks at me hard. His expression says, "I'm not playing."

I count to four before I speak. "What if Mookie and Shay Shay are yours, Cletus?"

"I'm going to claim them as mine. We'll go to court or welfare, or wherever we need to go to make it legit on paper. I'll pay child support, or maybe I'll marry their mother, once she becomes a Christian."

"Cletus! You sly fox, you! I *knew* you liked Angeleese! Have you two been seeing each other, like dating?" I'm happy for Cletus. He's done so well since he became a member of the church. I try to place my next words carefully. "Cletus, does she understand what it means to be a member of the church? Is she going to be baptized, though? The last I heard, she was afraid she'd drown in the baptistery."

"That's where you come in, NikkiMac. I need your help with this. You're one of her favorite people in the church, or out, for that matter. She trusts you. If you stand by the baptism pool during the baptism, where she can see you, she says she'll feel safe enough to go into the water. She's seen you do your lifeguard thing with the church kids at the Hetzels city pool during our Vacation Bible School field trips. As far as repentance is concerned, she wants to be forgiven of her past sins. She wants to do what's right. She believes in Jesus and she'll confess Him as the Son of God. She believes what the Bible says in Acts chapter 2, verse 38 and Matthew chapter 10, verse 32."

"Okay, okay, Cletus. Sounds like you and Angeleese have thought this through. Did you speak with Minister Johnson about this?"

"You know I did. He's eager to have her added to the kingdom of God, to have another soul saved."

"So, all you need for me to do is be with Angeleese at the baptism?" I notice that Cletus' left foot starts to tap before his mouth gives me a reply. "What's up with the foot tapping, Cletus?"

"There's just one more thing, NikkiMac." He looks at the ground, so I know something weird is about to come out of his mouth.

"At her baptism, Angeleese needs for you to have your lifeguard suit on and wear your lifeguard whistle. That way, she'll know you're ready to jump into the water and rescue her if the baptizing brother somehow lets her slip or keeps her under the water too long."

"You want me to wear my lifeguard uniform in church?" I allow myself a mental image of me in my bright orange, just-above-the-knee length stretchy lifeguard pants and equally vivid stretchy tank top. While the fabric does cover some of my cellulite sins, I'm not sure church is the right place to wear the outfit, even to help with Angeleese's baptism anxiety. "Cletus, can we at least do this after a Sunday service or meet at the church building with Brother Johnson? There won't be so many people then."

"Angeleese says she wants the church and her children to witness her baptism, along with the angels in heaven." Cletus says this sentence quite softly, like he expects me to haul off and coldcock him right upside his wooly head. I know I'm getting an attitude, because my right eyebrow arches and stays like that. Cletus must notice this arched strip of my facial hair, because he starts talking really fast.

"Please, NikkiMac, you know Angeleese is special. She thinks this is the only safe way to do this, and there's no amount of logic that can convince her otherwise. At least she's willing to live for the Lord and help her children learn about God. Do this for us, I'm begging you." For almost a minute, I remain silent. My personal discomfort at seeing my big orange-outfitted bottom in the baptistery with a whistle around my neck is weighed against seeing sweet, mentally challenged Angeleese being baptized into the church. God prevails, and I yield.

"Alright Cletus. When are we going to do this?"

"During tomorrow morning's worship service, NikkiMac." His voice is again at whisper level, and his eyes plead for my peaceful consent.

All of a sudden, the church door opens and Angeleese, with her five children in tow, dash outside. Angeleese asks Cletus, "Did NikkiMac say she would do it?" The children, who often seem to be in a chronologically ordered line, stand in place behind their mother. Scooter, Ziggy, Cha-Cha, Mookie, and Shay Shay look ready to celebrate. I'm about to have a heart attack because they scared the stew out of me, popping up like that. "Hey, NikkiMac! Please say you'll help me get baptized! I won't be afraid if you're there! Please?" Angeleese isn't much bigger than a middle school student, and her innocent charm makes it hard for me to deny her.

"Angeleese, I told Cletus I'd help out, not that I really get it, but because it's important to you."

"You're gonna wear your lifeguard suit, right? You may have to jump into the water to keep me from drowning!" Her pink, lip gloss-coated full lips and her tiny, bright teeth shine.

"Yes, I'll be dressed to save you, but I doubt the good Lord is going to let you die while you're going through the waters of baptism."

Angeleese's face lights up when she hears me agree to help her. She begins what appears to be a skipping dance of joy. Her children come alive and circle her, saying, "Yes, yes, yes!" Next, they break the circle, grab Cletus, and hug him around his legs with their little arms. I look at Cletus, who appears relieved that this part of the journey to the baptism of Angeleese is over. Yet, as he watches this gleeful woman and her children, there's another emotion on his face. He radiates warmth, tenderness, and care. Cletus gently reaches for Angeleese and embraces her while the children continue to chant and skip. Her eyes crinkle at the corners and she smiles. She stands on her tiptoes, looks up at Cletus, and wraps her arms around his shoulders. He gives her a quick kiss on the lips. The children applaud.

"Cletus is in love, God bless him," I say out loud as I shake my head and wonder what I've gotten myself into. Jacee approaches; she must be finished helping Poppa Pace.

"You know what they say about people who talk to themselves, NikkiMac."

"No, Jacee, but I'm sure you'll tell me."

"They say they're crazy, Girl."

"Well, you've known me for most of my life, so if you think I'm crazy, I must be. But check this out, you must be the same kind of crazy, though, since you hang out with me." We both laugh until I get serious. "Jacee, Angeleese plans on getting baptized tomorrow."

"That's wonderful! She finally got over her fear of drowning in the baptism water!"

"Let me finish, Jacee. She wants me by her side in case she somehow slips out of the baptizing brother's grasp and starts to drown." Jacee opens her mouth to respond. "I'm still not finished telling you. She wants me to wear my lifeguard outfit, complete with whistle, so I'll be ready to jump in and save her if she needs me. I guess she thinks the sound of the whistle will alert Jesus to her plight faster than anything else will."

My best friend since elementary school closes her large, hazel eyes, tilts her head back, and throws out laughter. Her noise is so loud that the three men shooting craps across the street stop and look our way.

One of them, Boopy, hollers to us. "Y'all okay over there, ladies? Y'all mighty loud to be in the churchyard. You gonna wake up Jesus with all that racket!" He laughs at his own joke.

Jacee stops laughing and hollers back. "We're fine, Boopy. Just so you know, Jesus doesn't sleep. He's always watching. Sorry to disturb your gambling session."

"Alright now, ladies, be breezy!" Boopy starts to shake the dice in his hands, and we recognize this as an end to our friendly verbal exchange.

Jacee says to me, "I'm surprised Boopy is sober enough to gamble. Remember the time he came to church drunk and offered Cletus a swig from his bottle? What a piece of work he is! He's probably trying to win enough to buy another bottle of that cheap rotgut they drink. Now, back to you, NikkiMac. Please tell me you're not wearing your stretchy orange lifeguard outfit to church tomorrow."

"Don't be silly, Jacee. I'm going to change into the outfit when I go into the dressing room with Angeleese. When she steps down into the water, I plan to stand far enough behind the curtain so only the baptizing brother and Angeleese will see me. I don't have a need for the congregation to see me dressed like that in church."

"At least your body's still tight, NikkiMac. Your gym workouts are working for you. Not bad for forty."

"Thanks, Jacee. If I were as naturally slim as you are, I wouldn't have to work so hard to keep it at 150 pounds."

"Yeah, but you've got the curves guys like."

"Don't even go there, Jacee."

"I hear you. There don't seem to be many prospects for single church ladies. Well, I've got to stop by my parents' house and then head home. Don't worry about the Angeleese baptism situation. You'll be fine. It might not make sense to us, but if it gets her into Christ, that's all that counts. I've got your back, my sister." We embrace each other. She gets into her car, and I get into mine. Angeleese's five children run over to Poppa Pace to watch him lock the churchyard gates for the night. When Poppa Pace secures the gates, Cletus and Angeleese beckon the children. As the children run from Poppa Pace to them, Cletus and Angeleese hold hands.

Chapter 13

Sunday Morning

The church radio program plays while I dress for Sunday morning service. The voice of our minister, Brother Johnson, urges the listeners to visit the congregation and hear more of the gospel of Christ. Next, our acapella group, *Praise*, sings *Say A Prayer*. The dynamic male soloist on *Say A Prayer* makes me feel like he's speaking for me, especially this morning. Angeleese had better get into the pool and get baptized this Sunday morning. I don't want to look like a fool in a lifeguard outfit for nothing. If she even looks like she's trying to back out, I'll throw her into the water myself. Somebody surely needs to say a prayer for me today. I catch a glimpse of my expression in the mirror and chuckle before I scold myself out loud, "Way to have a Christian spirit, NikkiMac! Now pack your lifeguard stuff and a positive attitude and get to church."

When I arrive, Darius Muse is about to enter the building, but he sees me and waits to hold the door open for me with his good arm. "Good morning, Sister NikkiMac. It's truly a pleasure to see you at church this morning." He smiles a little too brightly for my comfort. Every now and then, when I look at Darius, I still feel the unwanted press of his body against mine and the sting of his hand slap on my cheek. I try to check the unpleasantness and remember that he's a Christian now. He did ask for my forgiveness.

"Hello, Brother Darius. Thanks for holding the door for me. How are you today?" I keep it moving while I speak, because I feel like I have to.

"You're welcome, my sister. I'm still waiting for you to accept my invitation to join me for a cup of coffee one day after service."

I think, "It'll be a cold day in August before I'm ready to sit across from you and drink coffee or anything else," but I don't say it. Thankfully, some other members come along and engage Darius in conversation.

Change of clothes in hand, I find my seat and prepare my mind for worship. Jacee rushes in just before the bell rings. She winks at me and says, "You ready, NikkiMac? I saw Angeleese, Cletus, and her children in the lobby. They seem excited."

"They always seem excited, Jacee. I'm ready." I give her a wink so she'll know I'm okay.

Brother Flowers asks the congregation, "Are there any requests for prayer?" I cross my fingers and hope no one says anything strange, but hope flies out of the window when Sister Honey stands up.

"I have a request. Actually, I have something to say, because I'm mad as fire! For the last two weeks I wasn't at church because I was visiting my sister in the state of Virginia. When I got back home, there were sympathy cards at the house. I asked my brother, who goes to another church in Trenton, why people sent these cards. He was told someone here announced that I was dead. People called the house wanting to know when my funeral was! As you can plainly see, I'm fully alive." The whispers begin. I assume *The Position*: I place my right hand on my bowed forehead, lean forward, and slowly nod my head from side to side.

"I didn't hear anybody announce that here!"

"Ain't that a shame? Poor thing!"

"She better not be dead, 'cause she's right here talkin' as plain as day!"

Brother Flowers clears his throat. "Sister Honey, I don't think that announcement was made here. I certainly didn't make it. However, I did hear the rumor, and I believe someone who had good intentions but bad information started the rumor. I'm sorry for your discomfort, my sister. Church, before you pass along information about someone's demise, please verify it first. Whoever made the first phone call about this should have checked with our minister beforehand. Let's always consider each other the way we should. That's what the Bible tells us.

We're very thankful that you're still among the living, Sister Honey. Welcome back home from Virginia."

"Amen, brother."

"That's right."

Sister Honey seems to be satisfied with this, so she sits back down. The song leader starts off *Be With Me, Lord* and I think how appropriate this hymn is for what I'm about to do a short while from now. In the pew ahead of us sit Cletus, Angeleese, Scooter, Ziggy, Cha-Cha, and twins Mookie and Shay Shay. The children are all aglow. This is partly because they have so much petroleum jelly slathered on their little faces. I call it the poor folks' moisturizer. It works, but it does make you shine. Each time the children turn around to wave at me, I'm tempted to wipe some of the shine from their cute faces. Service continues with more songs, prayer, and scripture reading. My stomach gets a little tense every time I look at my tote bag containing my lifeguard outfit, but I'm determined to do what's necessary.

Following communion, my attention is somewhat diverted by a visitor who comes in with her baby and sits on the second pew. The child is attractive, but he has a high-pitched squeal, which his mother encourages by wagging her face in his face. Delighted, the baby responds with a squeal, right on cue. He sounds like a happy mouse on crack. The baby's mother ignores the sermon and plays with the baby like this until an usher speaks with her. I can't make out the words, but he appears to invite her and the baby to sit in the nursery, where we have a video monitor. That way, she can see and hear the service but not be a distraction. The visitor agrees and starts to move.

"I'm glad she took her silly self and the baby to the nursery," says Jacee.

"I know. Why would she sit up front and play with the baby and make him squeal like that? She could've stayed home, for all she's getting out of the worship service," I reply.

Jacee goes from the sublime to the ridiculous. "Maybe going to church is a condition of her parole."

"Shut up, Jacee." I notice her shoulders shake in laughter at her own joke. After we sing *Give Me The Bible*, Brother Johnson stands before the audience.

"It's truly a blessing to see everyone today. God watched over us last night as we slumbered and slept. Am I right about it?"

"Amen."

"He touched us with a finger of love and woke us up from our sleep. He gave us homes in which to get ourselves cleaned up and dressed for worship this morning. Isn't that right, church?"

"That's right!"

"Amen, brother!" The group response gets louder.

"No one in this room appears to be suffering from starvation this morning. That's because God provided food for us. I know some of us like to eat. Can I get a witness?" There's some chuckling and verbal affirmation.

"God even provided the transportation that got us to church service. Before that, God gave us the mind to come and worship Him in Spirit and in truth. Let's not take any of our blessings for granted. Let's remember to thank God for all He's done, what He does, and what He will do for us in the future. John chapter 3, verse 16 lets us know that God gave His Son for our salvation. What a sacrifice from our God!"

"Preach, Brother Johnson!"

"Hallelujah!"

"Amen! Thank you, Lord!"

"As a matter of fact, let's all sing the hymn *Praise Him! Praise Him!* The song leader starts off and we join him. After the song, Brother Johnson makes a few more remarks and soon concludes his message. Jacee can't let this pass unnoticed.

"NikkiMac, that must be the shortest sermon Brother Johnson's ever preached." I smile and shake my head while I think about what comes next: Angeleese's baptism. When we all stand to sing the invitation song, *Just As I Am,* Angeleese's children become animated, as if they expect a big event. Cletus looks at Angeleese, and then moves aside so she can exit the pew and start to walk down the aisle toward the preacher. Before she begins her first step in the aisle, she turns to me.

"You ready, NikkiMac? I need you to help me do this." If I had a thought about disappointing her, the thought went away once I saw the pleading look in her eyes.

"I'll see you by the baptism pool, Angeleese. It's going to be alright." I give her what I hope is a comforting smile. Angeleese proceeds to the front of the church to meet Brother Johnson. She reaches for his hands and holds them in hers.

"Praise God! This is truly wonderful! Miss Angeleese has been participating in church activities for quite some time, and she's been attending worship services. I want to point out that she brings her children to the church building with her, and this is a good example for some members. She doesn't come to church and leave her children home. Amen, church?"

"Amen, preacher!"

Brother Johnson continues, "Angeleese has decided to be baptized into Christ for the remission of her sins." He turns her to face the audience.

"Angeleese, if you believe this statement, please repeat it after me: I believe that Jesus Christ is the Son of God." He pauses for her response.

"I believe that Jesus Christ is the Son of God."

"Amen!"

"Praise the Lord!"

Many express joy at Angeleese's confession. She's here so often that she seems like family to most of us. Her five children clap with excitement. They may not fully recognize what's going on here, but they seem to understand that it's something good.

"Angeleese, this confession brought death to Christ, but will bring life to you after you've completed your obedience through baptism. You'll receive the gift of the Holy Spirit to help you live faithfully. Continue to worship and study the Bible and it will be well with your soul. Please follow Sister Longstreet to the dressing room, and she'll assist you with clothing for baptism." The two women begin to walk to the dressing room. Then, Angeleese stops, turns around, and looks at me.

Cletus taps me on my arm and whispers, "What are you waiting for, NikkiMac?" I grab my bag and join Angeleese and Sister Longstreet. The song leader begins the hymn *I Surrender All* as Angeleese and I change into our clothes for the water. In the baptism area, the curtain is positioned so that I'm visible only to Angeleese, Sister Longstreet, and the brother assigned to baptize for today. The baptism proceeds smoothly for Angeleese, who is fully immersed and is added to the body of Christ. The only problem is it turns out that Brother Adam Greene is the baptizer, so he gets to see me in my form-fitting orange lifeguard uniform, complete with the whistle around my neck. Oh, joy.

Chapter 14

Brother Oswald Stone

"Who's that brother, NikkiMac? I don't recognize him." We're early, so Jacee and I sit on the bench in the grassy area of the church parking lot, where we sometimes enjoy the breeze. The church doors will open in a few minutes.

"I don't think I've seen him before, Jacee. Oh! Poppa Pace has the man by the upper arm, like he's guiding him." I try not to stare, but I'm curious. The man is tiny. It looks like he's covering a slight frame under his large brown and black plaid sport coat and dark brown slacks, and I can tell by his face that he's older than me. His short Afro has flecks of gray, and his head is shaped like the top of an old style light bulb. He has the presence of a mature English professor, and he wears thick horn-rimmed eyeglasses. There's something about his eyes that I don't quite get right away. As they move closer to us, Jacee starts to say something to the two men, but I talk over her, because I know she hasn't thought first.

"Good morning, Poppa Pace. Good morning, brother," I say to the two men.

"Good morning, Daughter NikkiMac and Sister Jacee," says Poppa Pace. He hugs me and shakes Jacee's hand. Since Poppa Pace let go of the man's arm to greet Jacee and me, the man stands still as if he's not sure which way to move. Poppa Pace quickly returns his hand to the shorter man's arm. "Sisters, this is Brother Oswald Stone. Brother Stone, this is Sister Nikolis McQuaige, but she likes for us to call her Sister NikkiMac or just plain NikkiMac." Poppa Pace takes the hand of Brother Stone and guides it to my outstretched hand.

"Enchanted, Sister Nikolis McQuaige. No disrespect intended, but allow me this one time the pleasure of greeting you with your lovely given name. You must be aware that McQuaige is of Scottish heritage, my dear," says Brother Stone. He takes my hand, guides it to his lips, and kisses it ever so lightly before he releases it.

For a moment, I'm speechless, but I recover. "You're quite the gentleman, Brother Stone. I don't get that type of greeting every day. Yes, I'm aware of my last name's origin, and I'm proud to be a McQuaige. It's a pleasure to meet you also." I try to reach his gaze but note that his head is bowed a little and his eyes are closed behind the thick eyeglasses lenses. In another second, I get it. He's blind.

Not the one to miss an opportunity to put her foot in her mouth, Jacee blurts out, "Why do you have your eyes closed, Brother Stone? Is everything okay? Is something in your eye?" I elbow her.

Then, Brother Pace guides Brother Stone's hand to Jacee's. Brother Stone kisses Jacee's hand and replies, "It is also wonderful to meet you, Sister Jacee. Nothing's wrong, thank you, my dear. I lost my sense of sight long ago, but God has blessed me in so many other ways."

Brother Pace steps in before Jacee can ask more probing questions. "Brother Stone has a teaching assignment at a nearby university for a few months, so he plans to join our worship services. He has an apartment in town on East State Street. We're going inside now so I can get our brother seated."

"Okay, we'll speak with you later, Brother Stone."

I don't know why, but both Jacee and I wave at him like he can see us. Before he walks away with Poppa Pace, Brother Stone turns and says, "Sister NikkiMac, that's a lovely ring on your right hand. Is it a chalcedony quartz?" At first, Brother Stone's words make me think about my missing ring box. Then, I wonder how he even noticed the ring.

Perplexed, I reply, "Yes, it is, Brother Stone, a blue one." I finger my treasured high school graduation gift from my late parents.

He smiles a crooked smile, and I see the dimple form in his chin. "I thought so. At another time, I'll tell you how I knew that. It's all in the touch, my dear."

Jacee and I watch the two men walk out of earshot before she says, "Was that weird or what?"

"What's weird, Jacee? This isn't the first time you've met a blind person." I don't want to admit that I'm a little creeped out by Brother Stone, but not because he's blind.

"Please, NikkiMac, stop being cute. What's with the hand-kissing European gentleman routine, and how did he identify your ring when he can't see, and what was that cologne? I've never smelled that before."

"I don't know, it reminds me of some type of fragrance oil, Jacee, but it's combined with a pipe tobacco. There's something odd about him that has nothing to do with his vision." We eye each other and quietly move toward the doors of the church. Inside, I greet some members before I find my seat. All at once, Poppa Pace walks over.

"Daughter NikkiMac, is it okay for me move Brother Stone over here to sit with you and Jacee? He says he'd like to sit next to me because he feels comfortable with the way I guide him, but now I have to help some of the brothers with a plumbing emergency in the kitchen. Besides you, Jacee, and me, he hasn't met anyone else here."

I hesitate, but then nod my agreement. I cut my eyes at Jacee before she tries to open her mouth. Poppa Pace walks Brother Stone to our pew and seats him next to me.

"Thank you, my dear, for agreeing to let me sit with you. I feel more comfortable with you, Sister NikkiMac. See, I referred to you with the name you prefer. Is that better for you?" He smiles and moves his hand around until it makes contact with the back of mine. He pats my hand the way one pats the hand of a small child. Skin-crawly feelings start, and I try to shake them off. I get no play from Jacee; it appears she's got a slight attitude because I signaled her to be quiet a minute ago. She'll get over it.

I respond to Brother Stone, who's all up under me. I dwarf the little man. "Thank you for calling me NikkiMac. It's time for service to begin, Brother Stone." Then, I move my hand.

Before opening prayer, Brother Carlos asks, "Are there any prayer requests at this time?"

"Yes, Brother Carlos, I have a request." It's Sister Whines, and she's appropriately named. She attends worship service about once a month, and every time she shows up, she brings her sad tale of woe. "I want you all to pray for me because I'm having a hard time making ends meet financially. Instead of some of you coming to my assistance, you criticize me for buying a new car or moving into a nicer apartment. That's not the Christian thing to do. Some of you refuse me when I occasionally ask for a loan, so maybe you should pray for yourselves. I'm just having a hard time." She stops talking, but she doesn't sit. Instead, she begins to whimper and mop her face with a large handkerchief. Several people roll their eyes up in their heads because they're so familiar with her routine. I tense in response to Sister Whines' performance.

Brother Stone must sense something in me because he asks, "Sister NikkiMac, are you okay? Does this sister do this often? Has the church assisted her?" He sounds more curious than concerned.

"She does this about once a month, Brother Stone. Some of us have given her money, and some have loaned her money. Once she gets it, she doesn't even speak to you again until she needs something else."

"Sister NikkiMac, that's what I detect in her voice. I'm blind, and even I can see she's phony." Jacee stifles a laugh.

Brother Carlos lets Sister Whines do her thing for a couple more seconds, and then speaks. "Sister Whines, is there anything else?" His voice sounds sincere, but I know Carlos' zany sense of humor is lurking and is about to emerge unless he checks it. The Latino brother is growing stronger in the faith, but he sometimes can't resist seeing the humor in most situations.

Sister Whines stops crying when she hears Brother Carlos. "No, that's all. Please pray that I get help with my problems. Please pray that the true Christians here will give me the support I need."

Sister Lois says, "Amen." We pay her no mind because she says "Amen" to just about everything. She'd say "Amen" even if the preacher stood up and said, "Baloney!" No one else speaks, so Brother Carlos prays.

"Our Father in heaven, holy is your name. Thank you for bringing us here to worship You in spirit and in truth. Father, Sister Whines asks for help, and we pray that You bless her according to Your will, because You know her situation even better than she does. I pray the church will show Christian love to her and that she'll also show Christian love to others. Help us all be obedient to Your will. In Jesus' name we pray. Amen."

"Amen."

"Thank you, Lord."

I think I hear Sister Whines grumble, "What kind of prayer is that? Is Brother Carlos trying to say I don't show Christian love?" Brother Carlos looks straight at her, smiles, and moves from the pulpit. Brother Vincent comes forward and leads three songs. Then, we have scripture reading and communion before Brother Johnson starts the sermon.

"Please turn in your Bibles to Matthew chapter 13, verses 44 through 46. Here, we read the parable of the hidden treasure in a field and the parable of the pearl. Let's read the verses out loud." Brother Johnson starts reading and we join in.

"I'm going to title this message *Finding Your Treasure*. We know that a parable is a story told to teach a lesson, to illustrate a main point. In these parables, the main point is the value of being in God's kingdom. God's kingdom is such a treasure that we should be willing to pursue it with all our might."

"Amen!"

"Preach it!"

"God's kingdom is actually both in the now and in the future. I see some of you looking at me strange, but stay with me. In the current kingdom, we voluntarily come under the reign of God. He doesn't *force* any of us to yield to His will and worship Him. Look at Philippians chapter 2, verses 12 through 15. God's obedient children are encouraged by God's work in them. Although the faithful serve God with obedient hearts, there is still in the present kingdom a struggle between the flesh and the spirit. We miss the mark sometimes. In the future kingdom, when we realize the full manifestation, there will be no struggle with sin, no sickness, no injury, no death, no calamity, and no tears!"

"Hallelujah!'

"Praise the Lord!"

"And so, please don't be distracted by the world. There's nothing we acquire here that's worth the joy of what we acquire by being under God's reign. In fact, what we should value most is God's reign over our lives. I'll say it again, yield to God's control over your life now, because when Jesus returns, all *will* yield. Read this promise in Romans chapter 14, verses 11 and 12. That includes those who rejected Jesus Christ before the Day of Judgment."

"Tell it!"

"Amen!"

"Please turn to Philippians chapter 3, verses 7 through 11. Let's read together." Our voices flow as we read the words of Apostle Paul. "These inspired words remind us that even if the kingdom of God costs us everything, it's well worth it. Brothers and sisters, visitors and friends, ask yourself this question: Have I found my treasure? Am I truly in the kingdom of God?"

Next to me, Brother Stone is so much into the sermon that he waves his hand in support. Since he can't see, he hits the lady in front of him upside the back of her head. This knocks off her wide-brimmed hat and exposes her bounce back knots and BB shots.

"Ouch!" She grabs her head with one hand and retrieves her hat with the other.

"I'm so very sorry, Miss," says Brother Stone.

One of the teens nearby begins to snicker. This sets off a chain reaction, the next teenager elbows another, who jumps and slips off the pew. Thankfully, the song leader starts singing *Are You Washed In The Blood?* The ushers spring into action and caution the disruptive teens. I get Brother Stone situated, and Brother Johnson finishes the invitation. The vocal response shows that the audience is moved by the sermon. Next, the ushers collect the offering and we sing *What A Friend We Have in Jesus.* During the announcements, Brother Martin asks Brother Stone to stand, and I help him get up.

"Church, Brother Pace asked me to introduce Brother Oswald Stone. He'll be teaching at a nearby university, and he plans to worship with us for a while. Please offer him the right hand of fellowship."

Brother Stone clears his throat and says, "I am glad to be among such a fine group of Christians. Thus far, I've met Brother Pace, Sister Jacee, and Sister NikkiMac. I look forward to meeting many more of you. Thank you." I help him sit down.

"Amen."

"Welcome, brother!"

"Is he blind? He must be, his eyes are closed," one sister asks and answers her own question.

We have dismissal prayer. Folks begin to greet one another enthusiastically. I see Jacee make a beeline for Sister Chloe, and I wonder what that's about. Poppa Pace walks over after prayer and speaks with Brother Stone, then with me.

"Daughter NikkiMac, thanks for looking out for Brother Stone. I need to ask for your help again, if I may."

"Sure, Poppa Pace. What do you need?" I hope it has nothing to do with Brother Stone, but I'd help Poppa Pace no matter what. He's been good to me.

"I have to wait around for the plumber to finish up before I can lock the building. Will you ask Brother Leethan to give Brother Stone a ride home? That way, he won't have to sit around and wait for me."

"Sure, Poppa Pace, I'll take care of it."

I touch Brother Stone's shoulder before I speak to him. "I'm going to find Brother Leethan so he can give you a ride home. I'll be right back." Before I can take a step away from Brother Stone, he finds my hand and holds it.

"Sister NikkiMac, I'm not at all familiar with this Brother Leethan fellow. Would you please take me home?" The whiny quality of his voice makes him sound more like a scared little boy than a mature college instructor. This doesn't feel right to me. I wonder why he didn't say this in front of Poppa Pace.

"Where do you live, Brother Stone?"

"I live on East State Street, Sister NikkiMac." Do I now detect smugness in his tone? Slowly, he stands and offers his elbow so I can grasp it and lead him from the pew. As we make our way up the aisle, a few members speak to us. I notice a few curious expressions. Others give Brother Stone sympathetic looks.

"Tell me, Sister NikkiMac, am I getting looks of pity from these people?" My head jerks, and I'm glad he can't see me. He's like a mind reader.

"A few, Brother Stone, a few. Now, let's get you home." We get in my car and ride to a three-story brownstone on East State Street, where I park my car across the street because there's no parking allowed in front of his building. I notice the way he waits expectantly while I walk around the outside of my car to open the door for him and help him out.

"Grab my arm, dear," he instructs. I help him get out, then close and lock my passenger door. We move to the curb and pause for the traffic.

"There aren't many cars today," says Brother Stone. He must sense the question on the tip of my tongue, because he continues, "I can still hear the vehicles, even if I can't see them, my dear." We cross the street, climb his front steps, and he takes his front door key out of his jacket pocket. I watch as he feels the keyhole with his fingers and matches the key tip to the keyhole. He inserts the key, turns it, and opens the door. "Not bad for a blind man, huh?" His smile is broad but not infectious. I'm ready to go, and this fact makes me feel guilty. Using the banister, Brother Stone begins to climb the two full flights of stairs to his third floor apartment, with me following behind him. Along the way, he chatters in a cheerful manner.

"I enjoy taking the stairs because it keeps me fit, good exercise, you know." I look at my watch. It's one-thirty, and I have to eat, rest, and be back at church for the Sisters Class at five o'clock.

"Sister NikkiMac, I have some wonderful books you might be interested in borrowing. Of course, they're the Braille versions, but I can help you with that. You do like to read, don't you? Of course you must! I sense that about you." My eyes are drawn to his right pants pocket. There's a bulge inside. I hope it's not a gun.

"Perhaps you can escort me to the bank on a Saturday, Sister NikkiMac. I have a check that needs to be cashed. I think there's a branch of my bank in the area. We can go there early some Saturday morning."

Forget guilty, now I'm annoyed. Who does this blind man think he is? No, who does he think *I* am, his new personal assistant? We finally reach his apartment door, where he does the same routine with another key and the lock. The door opens to a small room with a couple of cushioned armchairs, a table, a lamp, and lots of books.

"Welcome to my little spot. Would you like me to give you a tour? Perhaps you can stay for a cup of tea."

"Brother Stone, I don't mean to be unkind, but now that you're home safely, I have to go. I need to take care of a couple of things before the Sisters Class and evening service."

"Perhaps I won't think of you as rude if you'll agree to pick me up for the evening worship service, my dear." He smiles in my direction. Is he flirting with me?

"Brother Stone, I'll ask Brother Pace to handle that." My attitude is funky because I feel like he's using his blindness to take advantage of me. My voice must show how I feel, because he backs off.

"Oh, I apologize if I've offended you, Sister NikkiMac."

I move to the apartment door. "No problem, Brother Stone. I'll see you later." I close the door and zip down the two flights of stairs as if the little blind man is in hot pursuit.

Chapter 15

A Date With a Preacher

It's Friday night, and according to the clock on the mantle, it's six o'clock. I'm glad for the weekend, because my students have been very antsy this week, and the administration has introduced yet another innovation they want the teachers to implement. At a recent staff meeting, a consultant presented the latest thing to come down the pike. A fifth grade teacher said, "If they had to try and make these cockamamie ideas work with the children, maybe the administration would think twice about actually adopting them!" Many of the teachers agreed. I feel like having some company, so I call Jacee. She picks up on the third ring.

"Hey Sis, what's going on with you tonight? Want to go see a movie?"

"Hi, NikkiMac! You bet I would, but my mother called a few minutes ago. She wants me to drive her and my dad to her sister's house in Newark for a family dinner. Dad doesn't see well enough to drive at night anymore, especially on Route 1, so they asked me. Why not come with us?"

"Is your make-believe uncle, Mr. Gus, going to be there?" I picture Jacee's overly friendly fake relative with the big belly and boozy breath. He likes to squeeze the meat on the back of my arms and tell me how "fluffy" I am.

Jacee laughs, but I don't find this funny. "NikkiMac, he's a harmless old man. Squeezing your arms is probably the biggest thrill he gets these days! Besides, he hangs around my family so much he most likely thinks he's a real relative."

"Thanks, but no thanks, Jacee. I'll take a pass. Maybe next time, when I feel like giving out sympathy squeezes. See you later. Smooches."

I hang up and decide to make a cup of tea and read some fiction. On my way to the bookshelf in the living room, I notice car headlights through the window in the front of the house. I wonder who's parking way down here near the end of the street. I'm not expecting anyone. I reach the living room and turn off the ceiling light so I can peek through the blinds without being seen. There's a dark-colored sports car across the street from my house, right in front of the empty lot. There's a driver inside and the smoke from the tailpipe tells me the car's engine is running. Wait, the headlights just went out! As I kneel on my small bench so just the top of my head is visible from outside, I take slow, deliberate breaths. Does this have anything to do with that dream I had about an intruder? A bright flash from a cigarette lighter and the resulting glow of a cigarette tip reveal that someone's having a smoke in the car. By the size of his head, the driver appears to be a man. I strain my eyes to make identification, but the profile is unrecognizable. Now, the smoker turns his head and looks directly at my house. Does he see my head in the window? My brain seesaws. The abrupt, brighter glow of his cigarette tells me he's taking a final, deep drag. The car window glides down and his hand pushes out and releases the still glowing cigarette butt to the street. Like a snake in retreat mode, the hand slides back inside the car. The window glides back up. There's a brief side view of the man's head again before the car pulls off and heads to the corner of Taylor and Poplar Streets. There, it makes a right onto Taylor Street and I watch the taillights grow smaller and smaller as the car moves out of my sight. I decide I'm being paranoid. Just because a person smokes a cigarette in a car across the street from my house, it doesn't mean he's a menace.

All of a sudden, my phone rings. The shrill sound makes me jump from my knees to my feet so fast that I bump my head on the windowsill. "Ouch!" I holler, as I feel around in the dark room for the light switch. I find it, flip it up, and light appears. I grab the phone. "Hello, McQuaige residence. NikkiMac speaking."

"Hello, Sister NikkiMac. This is Brother Adam Greene calling." I can't believe my ears! Thoughts about the mysterious car across the street fly away from my mind. Right now, I've got better thoughts to think. I picture Adam's dark, chocolaty skin, those earnest, green eyes, and his lean, tall frame.

"Who did you say this is?" For a moment, I don't trust my hearing. It could be playing a trick on me.

"It's Brother Adam Greene. Do you have a minute, or should I call back later?" I get myself together, because I'd have to be totally out of my mind to postpone a call from this man.

"Brother Adam, it's good to hear from you. What can I do for you?" As soon as I say that, I regret it, because I sound like a saleswoman or a hooker.

"Well, Sister NikkiMac, a while ago, I asked you for your phone number because I have a question for you. I made the decision to call tonight because it's very important to me." Maybe he wants me to work with him and some other members on another church project, although he did say it was personal when he brought this up in the first place. I try not to get excited, because I don't want to be disappointed. I use my professional tone.

"Yes, Brother Adam, please ask your question."

"Are you single, or dating anyone, Sister NikkiMac?"

I catch my breath. Has he heard some lie that he feels he needs to address with me? It would have to be a lie, because I haven't been with anybody since Alex, and he checked out on me a while ago.

"Brother Adam, I'm single. I'm not dating anyone. I haven't dated anyone in quite awhile."

"That's good to hear." He sounds relieved and encouraged.

"You're not dating because you don't want to date? Or is it that you haven't met anyone you care to date?"

"It's very difficult to meet mature single Christian men, men who are serious about dating according to the principles found in scripture. I decided to wait on the Lord. He handles my life better than I do. It would be wonderful to meet a like-minded brother, and I do get lonely sometimes. I just pray about it and keep myself busy."

"Sister, I've noticed that you spend a lot of your energy and talent with the church youth and education programs. You do good work, many folks are blessed by your efforts."

"Thank you, Brother Adam. Now, it's my turn to ask you a question or two." I feel my boldness return. "Why do you want to know about my relationship status?" I can't believe I'm having this conversation with Brother Adam; the assistant minister with the kind heart and strong dedication to the Lord. He actually stutters as he delivers his bottom line.

"Sister NikkiMac, I—I—I would like to ask you out on a proper date." Before I answer, I do a silent dance of thanks around my living room. I know I must look like I'm in a stage production of some musical, but I really don't care.

"I'd like that, Brother Adam." All that dancing makes me sound a little breathy.

"Great! Are you okay? You're breathing harder all of a sudden." I can hear concern in Brother Adam's voice.

"He's such a sweetness!" is what my late mother, Alice, would have said about him.

"I'm fine, Brother Adam. When would you like to go out?"

"How about tonight? We could catch the next show at the AMC Theater in Hamilton, grab some food and a cup of coffee or tea at a local place, and share some conversation. I can have you back home before midnight. I know this is last minute, and I'll understand if you have other plans. It's just that I've found the courage to ask you, so I'm jumping on it."

I start to perspire. I feel like I'm having a hot flash, and I'm not even menopausal yet. I cover the phone's mouthpiece with my hand and whisper, "Thank you, Jesus. You sent me a good Christian man to date, and a *fine* one at that!"

"It's a good idea, Brother Adam. Let's go out tonight. I can be ready in fifteen minutes."

"I'll be right there, Sister NikkiMac."

"Brother Adam, how do you know where I live?"

"Your address is in the church directory, remember? Plus, I asked Brother Johnson for the directions to your house. I hope you don't mind, Sister NikkiMac."

"It's cool, Brother Adam. I guess since we're going out on a date, I can call you Adam, right?"

"You guessed right, and I can call you NikkiMac. See you soon." The phone clicks off on his end. I stare into space, and then spring into action. I run upstairs to my bedroom, where I grab outfits from the closet and fling them left and right across my bed.

"No, this looks like a corny school teacher." Toss.

"Maybe, but I don't know if I want to wear pants." Toss.

"This top is a great color for my complexion, but it's there's too much cleavage action going on here." Toss.

"Why did I ever buy this dress?' Toss.

"This skirt makes my backside look big. Everything makes my backside look big. I can't believe I'm having this conversation with myself out loud! Stop it, NikkiMac!" I count to ten to calm myself. Then, I reach for a nice pair of black denim jeans, a freshly pressed white cotton shirt, and a black tailored denim jacket. I slip on a pair of leather pumps and turn to check myself out in the full-length mirror. Not too shabby, fashionable, but not overdone. It's Friday night, after all, and this is a casual date. I go into the bathroom to beat my face in the mirror. Not much makeup, just a little powder and blush, some mascara and a bit of peach gloss on my lips. I smile at my brown freckles, my signature facial markers. My bangs work with me and hang just right above the thick eyebrows on my forehead. The bangs aren't flat and pressed up against the skin, instead they roll out with the hint of bounce. The sides of my hair touch my shoulders, while the back of my hair hangs longer, almost to the middle of my back. Silver hoop earrings shimmy in my lobes. Two silver pendants, a key and a heart, hang from a sterling chain and rest on my skin just above my shirt collar opening. "Not bad for my age," I say to my reflection.

The doorbell rings. Something in my stomach flutters, but my feet find control and take me downstairs. I look through the window and gaze at the frame of Brother Adam Greene, softly illuminated by the front porch light. He looks as scrumptious as a large box of expensive chocolates. Adam realizes I'm peeking at him and laughs. "Are you going to open the door or just keep eyeballing me, NikkiMac?" His voice is soft, but strong. As I open the door, my hands shake a little.

"Hello, Adam. Please come inside while I get my purse." He enters, and I breathe in his cologne. It smells crisp and fresh, with a hint of lime. I like it.

"I hope I didn't rush you, NikkiMac. Thanks so much for accepting my last minute invitation." What he probably doesn't realize is how thrilled I am that he called to ask me out. I'm leery about dating men outside the church because I want to avoid the intimacy issue. Although, according to statements from some of the single sisters, a few of the brothers in church appear to ignore what the Bible says about privileges acceptable in marriage only. I've been on the receiving end of remarks by certain frisky men in the church, and I cut those brothers off quickly. Anyway, tonight, I look forward to having some plain old good fun with Adam.

"Thanks for asking me out, Adam. I'm ready." We step outside, I lock my front door, and we walk to his car. He opens the door for me and makes sure I'm comfortably seated inside. Adam closes the door, walks to the driver's side, and lets himself in.

"You look nice, NikkiMac."

"Thanks, Adam." He drives away from the curb and carefully watches the road. At first, my eyes glance at his profile. Then, I close them and say a silent prayer of thanksgiving to God. He's given me an opportunity to spend some personal time with a faithful, eligible Christian man.

At the AMC Hamilton Theatre, I discover that Adam's the type of person who watches a movie in silence. That's cool with me. The movie has lots of suspense. When one of the characters hides behind a door and jumps out to attack another character, I grab Adam's hand.

"Oh, I'm sorry, Adam!" Embarrassed, I quickly release his hand.

"That's alright, NikkiMac." He smiles at me and returns his attention to the movie screen. After the movie, we stop at a coffee shop. Adam chooses an herbal tea, while I opt for a decaf hazelnut coffee.

"NikkiMac, thanks for being so cool about my choice of a 'guy movie' for tonight. You're a good sport. On our next date, feel free to choose the movie we see. I promise to make no complaints."

"On our next date? I like the sound of that. It's a deal, Adam."

"In the time I've been with the Trenton congregation, I've noticed several things about you that impress me. That's why I wanted us to get together and talk. A while back, you had a situation involving Tasha, Brother Pace's daughter." My stomach tightens, and I rest my cup of coffee on the table. "NikkiMac, it took a lot to publicly admit that you failed to help her. You repented and made a confession."

"Adam, God saw what I did. It was wrong, and I had to deal with the consequences of my behavior."

"That's my point, NikkiMac. Some Christians try to cover their sins, but you owned it and asked for forgiveness. You showed respect for God."

"Adam, I'm learning more about yielding to the Holy Spirit." As the evening progresses, Adam mentions my role in Angeleese's baptism, my work with the children, my supportive friendship with Cletus, and the time we went knocking on doors in the church evangelism outreach. I'm stunned to learn that Adam has been paying attention to me, and I didn't even notice it. Too soon, it's time to leave. Adam proves to be a man of his word. I'm back home by eleven forty-five. He walks me to my door, gives me a sweet, quick hug, and returns to his car. God is good.

Chapter 16

Wedge

Jacee takes a sip of her tea. As usual, she licks the outside surface of the teacup on her way to getting the liquid into her mouth. It's one of her familiar mannerisms that I no longer tease her about. She no longer teases me about the way I squint my eyes whenever I'm in deep thought. We're hanging out at my house before she visits her parents. I have the feeling she wants to tell me something, but I don't press her. As it often does, our conversation turns to our early days growing up in this East Trenton neighborhood. After Jacee swallows another sip of her tea, she speaks. "NikkiMac, remember Roxanne from up the street? She had the little brother who could dance his behind off! Whenever we sang a hit song, his little feet moved like lightning! He danced like a tiny James Brown!"

"Yep, Jacee. I remember Roxanne and her dancing little brother. How's she doing?"

"She still works for the state, and she looks good, too. Someone I haven't seen from back in the day is Wedge, and I'm glad about that fact. He was crazy like that, wasn't he, NikkiMac?"

"He sure was different, and don't forget his sidekick, Mar-Mar. If Wedge told Mar-Mar to jump off a rooftop, Mar-Mar would do it. That's how much he followed behind Wedge. I believe following Wedge is what got Mar-Mar killed, but nobody around here talks about it."

Jacee shakes her head in agreement. "Well, NikkiMac, I hate to break up our trip down Memory Lane, but I've got to visit my folks."

"Thanks for stopping by. Give your parents a hug for me." I walk her outside and watch until she gets into her car and drives off. While

I wash our cups and saucers, I reflect on our earlier conversation about this neighborhood and the children who grew up here with us. Only a few of us still live in the Poplar Street, Tyrell Avenue, Hart Avenue, Hurley Street, Taylor Street, Oak Street, Dickinson Street, and North Clinton Avenue area. Most of our old acquaintances and friends ended up in other parts of the city or out of town. In fact, I can account for the whereabouts of all of them except one: Wedge. It's interesting that his name came up earlier tonight. Some people are hard to forget, and not necessarily because they leave behind fond memories.

My thoughts travel again to Wedge, who was truly a character back in our early East Trenton days. I don't know if Wedge was his first name, maybe it was his last name, but it's the only name for him we knew. We never saw his parents; his Grandpa Joe raised him. Wedge usually wore a sweatshirt, jeans, and high top sneakers. He dressed that way during all four seasons, so he was particularly funky in the summertime. He always had a pair of taped up black binoculars in his back pocket. Wedge was thick, but not fat. He was solid, and taller than the rest of us, and he was actually handsome, in a frontier sort of way. He had dark, piercing eyes, heavy eyebrows, a thin nose, and a chiseled chin. His skin was the color of butterscotch pudding, and he had a head full of curly hair. His full lips covered bright white teeth. But there was craziness about him, an aura that warned one not to be deceived by his looks. His presence suggested both danger and intrigue. Often, when Wedge came through the old McClellan School yard, someone would holler, "Whoop, whoop, whoop!" and children would scatter. Nothing ruined a fun game of Hide and Seek like receiving a punch in the face from Wedge.

Mar-Mar was Wedge's flunky, and he'd take a beating for the privilege to fight alongside Wedge. Most of us avoided Wedge, but Mar-Mar didn't seem to talk to anybody *but* him. The rest of us neighborhood kids were at least a little afraid of Wedge, because we never knew what would set him off. When that happened, he'd haul off and punch you so hard that it was reported you'd see stars. One minute, he'd smile at you. The next minute brought his flashing eyes and granite fist. It didn't even matter if you were a girl. I never got punched, and I made a conscious effort to stay out of his way. Unpredictable people have always disturbed me.

My childhood problem with Wedge was that he took a liking to me, in a romantic way. He liked to pull my ponytails. I guess he thought it was a show of affection, but I detested it. He embarrassed me by telling the boys around our way, "Don't none of you dudes mess with Nikolis, or I'll jack you up! Don't nobody bother her; I got her back. One day she gonna be my girlfriend!" Every time he said it, I cringed. He'd often get in my face and say, "Girl, I got feelings for you. You got feelings for me?" I usually said I liked him a little bit, and then looked for a way to escape into my house. I frequently lied and said I heard my mother calling me.

Wedge and Grandpa Joe didn't intimidate most of our parents, who told us to stay away from them. My parents were prepared to take matters into their own hands if need be. For reasons I still can't explain, a lot of us kids didn't report Wedge's actions to our parents unless we felt we really had to. Were we that afraid of him? Or was it that we admired his toughness? Although he bullied us, he was the one who fought for us when boys from North Trenton or the Wilbur section came onto our East Trenton turf. As soon as these intruders crossed the invisible, but understood, boundary line, one of our lookouts would holler, "Go get Wedge! These dudes ain't got no business comin' around here!" Like a superhero, Wedge would appear, with Mar-Mar right behind him. It made no sense for the enemy to try and outrun Wedge. He was the fastest runner in the neighborhood. He'd always catch the biggest trespasser and knock him out. The rest would scatter. In a way, Wedge was our champion. He wasn't afraid of anything or anyone.

Next to punching people out, Wedge enjoyed stoning neighborhood cats and making dogs bad, or tough. He accomplished this by boxing the dogs' heads and pulling their tails. When they snapped at him, he bopped them with a stick. Anytime anyone reported Wedge's antics to his elderly grandfather, the old man cursed them out.

"Why every time something happen in this neighborhood, you people blame it on my grandson? Y'all get on my *bleeping* last nerve with that *bleep!* Get outta my face with that mess!" A wad of dark brown chewing tobacco juice punctuated the end of his sentences. When Grandpa Joe rolled the tobacco spit around in his toothless mouth, a wise person backed up and got out of the way.

Wedge and Grandpa Joe lived on Hart Avenue, not too far from Jacee's parents. Jacee told me that the residents on Hart Avenue left

Grandpa Joe and Wedge alone. Some say Wedge used to peek in the neighbors' first floor windows and climb a tall tree in his yard so he could look into the rear second floor windows on Poplar Street. Maybe that's why he always carried the beat up old binoculars.

When I was in the seventh grade, Wedge and four other boys allegedly pulled a train on Barbette. Wedge was said to have been the ringleader who came up with the plan. Folks say it happened in the graveyard, a lot between Hart Avenue and Oak Street. As children, we were told this lot was an actual ancient burial ground for Native Americans. I didn't play there much because my parents told me not to. Anyway, Wedge supposedly gave Barbette a dollar and she went into the bushes, laid down on a coat, and the boys took turns doing the *nasty* to her. Nobody did anything about it. That's because Barbette was a fast girl who did the *nasty* even when nobody paid her any money.

I guess Wedge was about my age, but he didn't go to elementary school, junior high school, or high school with the rest of us neighborhood kids. Folks said he went to a special school. Nobody teased him about riding the short yellow bus, though. Wedge and Grandpa Joe disappeared from the neighborhood while I was in Trenton High School. Some say they beat a person to death with a board, and I suppose they went to jail for that. All that was long ago.

The doorbell chimes and interrupts my thoughts about the past. I walk to the front room and look through the window. It's Jacee.

"Hey Sis, I'm back. NikkiMac, I need to share something with you." I quickly open the door for her.

"Jacee, what's going on? I knew something was on your mind. I figured you'd tell me about it when you were ready."

Jacee sighs. "NikkiMac, remember I told you a while back that I was going to apply for a special program that will let me attend graduate school and earn a Masters degree, along with supervisory certification? Well, I applied, and I got accepted into the program with a full grant."

"Congratulations, Jacee! I know you want to branch out in your career. We both plan to do that at some point, but why didn't you say something to me sooner? You know I'm your cheerleader!" I'm really puzzled that she didn't let me in on this earlier, because we usually talk about everything. Something more is definitely up. I gesture for Jacee to sit with me on my large sofa. She twists strands of her Afro, takes a deep breath, and begins to speak.

"NikkiMac, the problem is that I have to go to the graduate school they select, and the grant is for a school in Texas. They have an accelerated program that I can finish in a year and a half if I attend full-time. The award provides for housing, food, books, and tuition. It also allows me to have a paid job on campus. That will help with my personal expenses. I can sublet my apartment here in Trenton. Given that this is a unique initiative brought into the district by our superintendent, I can get a special leave of absence. When I'm finished with my degree, I'll be appointed to a supervisory position in the district's upcoming teacher mentoring program. I have to leave before the end of this school year." Jacee finally takes a pause. I look into the eyes of my best friend and see excitement mixed with sadness.

"What am I supposed to say? I'm happy for you, but why'd you wait so long to tell me all this? You're moving all the way to Texas for eighteen months?"

"NikkiMac, sorry for keeping quiet about this. I didn't want to get my hopes up in case I wasn't one of the five Trenton teachers selected. I just got the acceptance letter a couple of days ago."

It's not her news that hurts. It's the fact that she didn't feel like she could tell me about all this from the start. I clasp my hands and put them in my lap. After a few seconds, I unclasp my hands, move closer to my dear friend, and give her the supportive hug I know she needs.

Chapter 17

Brother Stone Strikes Again

I'm at the bank on a Saturday morning with Brother Stone and a bad attitude. Since I took him home a few weeks ago, I've pretty much been able to avoid him. He can't see me, after all. However, I'm a little hot under the collar about what he did last Thursday night following the *How to Study the Bible* class. He asked me to take him to the bank this morning. The way he did it perturbed me, because he asked one of the teenagers to bring me over to him. That's when he cornered me, right in front of young Chastity. He reminded me that he needed to get to the bank. He said I'd agreed earlier to take him. He smiled sweetly, but I felt a pushiness coming from him. Young Chastity watched us carefully. What was I supposed to say? I agreed to take him, and Chastity smiled. She probably figured I was showing the kindness that I teach about in our Bible classes.

So, here I am at the bank, the last place I want to be early on a Saturday morning. I don't even remember the last time I was inside this bank, because I have direct deposit and use online banking. Brother Stone now asks me to place his hand where he needs to sign the back of his check.

"I just need to mark an *X* on the name line and show my identification." He gives me his wallet and asks me to take out his identification card. I hand the card and his check to the teller.

"Good morning, Mr. Stone. How are you today?" Her nametag says she's Stella.

"I am fine, dear, especially since I have my extraordinary friend escorting me today." He finds my hands and pats them. I manage to smile for the teller.

"I'll have this for you in a moment." She spins away to do her thing on the bank's computer.

"Sister NikkiMac, you've lost weight, haven't you?"

"I don't know, Brother Stone, I haven't weighed myself in two weeks. Where'd you get that idea?"

"I can tell from your hands. I remember how they felt when I met you and when you took me home that time. Your hands now feel smaller, less plump, if you will." He smiles broadly, like he's figured out the answer to the million-dollar question. I am fed up! This man pays a little too much attention to me for my comfort level, and I don't care what he says about my plump or less plump hands.

"Brother Stone, I guess I could take that as a compliment." I try to be nice, but I know I need divine assistance, because this cheesy little blind man is getting on my nerves. He must sense my discomfort, because he changes the topic.

"My dear, you're escorting an unsighted man, but we're not without protection. Don't you worry about that at all, Sister NikkiMac. I have that covered." He pats the bulk in one of his pockets.

"What's that, Brother Stone? Please tell me it's not a gun." All I need is for a blind man with a gun to start shooting it near me.

"I assure you that my weapon is more effective than a gun, my dear." From his pants pocket, he pulls a small billy club wrapped with black electrical tape. "I've done some damage with this when I've needed to." He slaps the club into the palm of his hand. I'm not assured of anything other than the fact that I'm about to be freaked out.

Fortunately, the teller returns with Brother Stone's cash. He quickly slips the weapon back into his pocket.

"Here you are, Mr. Stone." Following his directions, she counts out the paper money in twenties, tens, fives, and ones.

"Please hand the bills to my companion," he says. When she does so, he and I move to a table.

"Sister NikkiMac, fold the twenties first. I need them folded in half before they're placed inside my wallet." I do as he says.

"Next, fold the ten dollar bills lengthwise. Then, fold the upper right corner of the fives. Finally, leave the ones unfolded. You see, this is my system for managing the money in my wallet." I take my time and follow his directions. After he checks that I've completed the task to his satisfaction, he puts his wallet away. We're now ready to leave the bank.

"Brother Stone, do we need to make any more stops before I take you back to your place?" I silently pray that he wants to go straight home, and my prayer is answered. I get him back to East State Street, help him out of my car, walk him up the steps to his apartment, and watch him get inside. As I turn to descend the stairs, Brother Stone calls out.

"Thank you ever so much, Sister NikkiMac. You know, I should have asked you to take me to the produce stand on North Clinton Avenue while we were out. Oh well, I'm sure Brother Pace will take me when he comes by later with the rest of my groceries." I say nothing, but I bolt down the stairs. I need to get away before I say something mean. I'm bothered by the fact that he'd even consider me running around with him when he knew someone else was coming by later to help him. I'm annoyed, yet I'm ashamed to feel this way. God wants me to help others in need, and He wants me to do so with a loving, compassionate spirit. When I get into my car, I pray for forgiveness for my attitude. I ask God to help me control my negative reaction to Brother Stone, and show me how to be a better person. Still, I have a nagging feeling that Brother Stone is taking advantage of me and will do so until I stop it. I have to do it the Christian way, though.

I decide to drive by the church building before going home. I'm relieved to see Poppa Pace sweeping the churchyard. I drive into the parking area and wave at him.

"Hello, Daughter NikkiMac! It's good to see you. What brings you by here?" I love the fact that Poppa Pace always seems genuinely pleased to see me. He gives me one of his comforting hugs.

"Poppa Pace, you're just the person I need to talk to right now. I'm so frustrated I could spit!" His brow furrows, and I can sense his protective nature.

"What's wrong, Daughter NikkiMac? Did somebody bother you?"

"Poppa Pace, did you know that Brother Stone asked me to take him home the first Sunday he came here with you? He knew you asked Brother Leethan to take him, but he wanted me to do it." Poppa Pace rests the broom against the churchyard fence.

"No, I didn't know that. I make a point of asking men, not women, to escort folks home, especially those folks who need special assistance, like Brother Stone."

"Poppa Pace, when I first met Brother Stone, something about him gave me the creeps. So, when I saw how he maneuvered me to take him home that Sunday, I kept my distance. Even on that Sunday, he wanted me to come inside his apartment and stay for a while. Another time, he had one of the teenagers bring me over to him so he could ask me to take him to the bank. I don't mind helping others. I know that's the right thing to do, but he says some things that make me feel uneasy. I'm not going so far as to say he's fresh, but it's more like he thinks he's courting me. I don't know how to explain it, Poppa Pace, but I don't feel comfortable with it."

"I don't like the sound of this, Daughter NikkiMac." Poppa Pace begins to show that storm cloud look on his face, the one he had when he protected me from Darius Muse all those years ago. "Four brothers in the congregation besides me agreed to assist Brother Stone, and he knows that. He has no business asking a sister to take him home, especially at night. These men have agreed to take him to and from church as well as assist with his errands. In fact, I'm going to his apartment later to drop off his groceries. I'll tell you one thing, he won't ask you again."

"Poppa Pace, I don't want to cause trouble for Brother Stone." Now, I feel bad.

"You're not the cause of anything, and there won't be any trouble. Don't worry about it. I've got it covered. Go on about your business. Enjoy the rest of your Saturday, Daughter NikkiMac." He gives me another hug, picks up the broom and resumes sweeping. I've been dismissed.

Chapter 18

Love Is In The Air

Sunday evening service is over, and as we walk out of the auditorium and approach the parking lot, Jacee taps me on my shoulder. "Check it out, NikkiMac!" I hear the mischief in her voice, which means she spies something or someone worth noting. I start to turn my head, but stop when she says, "Not now, don't look right now!"

"Jacee, make up your mind! Do you want me to see something, or don't you?" She's such a drama queen sometimes.

"Okay, look near the back church gate and see who's getting into Brother Foster Pace's car." I follow her directions and watch my Poppa Pace gently guide Sister Lovey Grace into the front seat of his car. Her lovely silver hair and her charming smile attract attention. Poppa Pace checks to be sure that the hem of her dress is tucked inside the car before he closes the door. Even from a distance, I detect something more than Poppa Pace's usual well-mannered behavior. There's a type of tenderness, and judging by the expression on both of their faces, it goes both ways.

"Wow, Jacee! I think they really like each other! When did all this happen?"

"Who knows? I think it's wonderful when two older Christians who've lost their mates get together and enjoy each other's company. Maybe that means there's hope for middle aged people like us."

"Jacee, we don't know if they're dating each other. It could be he's simply giving Sister Grace a ride home." I hope Poppa Pace has found a good Christian woman to join him in his older years. However, I feel weird about the fact that Poppa Pace didn't tell me he was actually interested in one of the church sisters. Not that he had to, of course, he's a grown man and doesn't need to report to me. Jacee looks at me with disbelief.

"Uh, uh! I know you're not getting an attitude because Brother Pace found someone else to enjoy his time with in a role other than NikkiMac's guardian angel. Get over yourself, NikkiMac."

"That's not what I feel, Jacee. You're so wrong. You need to take that back. It's just that Poppa Pace and I are so close and we share so many confidences that I'm surprised he never mentioned anything about dating Sister Grace. That's all." I think, but don't say, "Just like you, Jacee, and your waiting so long to tell me about your move to Texas."

"NikkiMac, are you sure it isn't mostly you sharing your confidences and problems while Brother Pace does the listening and counseling?" This is how I know Jacee is my best friend. No one else can talk to me like this without receiving a snappy retort and cool rebuff.

"Alright, alright, Jacee. You made your point. I'll get over myself." As Poppa Pace and Sister Grace ride out of the parking lot, they smile and wave at us. Before I can collect my thoughts, Cletus, Angeleese, and her five children show up.

"NikkiMac! Jacee! Wait up! We've got news!" Cletus appears quite content. Jacee frowns, because she still has issues with Cletus and his sincerity. She needs to get over *herself* about those issues.

"NikkiMac, we got the DNA testing. The twins are mine!" Cletus blurts this out like it's the best news in the world.

"Uh huh, NikkiMac. Cletus is they daddy, like I been telling everybody!" Angeleese beams like she just won the lottery.

Twins Mookie and Shay Shay skip around in a circle. They clap their hands and repeat, "Daddy! Daddy!" The older children look happy, too. Maybe they think their fathers will step up to the plate also.

Angeleese hugs me. "NikkiMac, God answered my prayer. Now Cletus knows he the twins' daddy for sure! We're gonna make plans for child support and everything. We might just end up being a family!" Jacee keeps quiet. I return Angeleese's hug and keep my mouth shut. I consider the difficulties she and Cletus will face if they marry and Cletus takes on the responsibility for all five of the children, even the three that aren't his. Cletus wears a proud expression.

"Cletus and Angeleese, I'm so happy for you and the children. Let me know if there's anything I can do to help."

"Oh, NikkiMac, you already did something good for me. I probably wouldn't be baptized and a Christian except for you." I smile and try to erase the memory of me in my swimsuit at Angeleese's baptism. She really is sweet, and a lot nicer than many people I know. The Bible lets us know that God can make things possible for His children. I'm sure He can help Cletus and Angeleese work this all out according to His will.

"We gotta go now. We just wanted to tell you the good news!" The two adults gather the children and they exit the parking lot.

"Off goes the little tribe," remarks Jacee.

"You sure were quiet while they were here, Jacee."

"What was there for me to say, NikkiMac? I'm not always successful, but I'm trying to let God guide my tongue and my heart. Cletus hustled folks for so long that I still sometimes have trouble believing he's changed, but that's not for me to talk to him about. I'm not trying to lose my salvation behind a bad attitude toward Cletus or anyone else."

"I know that's right, Jacee!" We hug each other and part. We've both got school paperwork to do before tomorrow morning.

Later that evening, as soon as I settle down for a cup of hot tea, the phone rings. It's Poppa Pace. "Hello, Daughter NikkiMac, how are you? Do you have a minute?"

"I'm fine, Poppa Pace. I always have a minute for you. What is it?"

"It's good news, NikkiMac, so I won't beat around the bush telling you. For the past few weeks, I've been keeping company with Sister Lovey Grace. She's a fine Christian woman, very easy to be around. She's been a widow for several years; she and her husband had no children. Daughter NikkiMac, she's so attentive to me. When we go out to the diner for coffee and tea, she watches to see if I like my cup of coffee before she settles into enjoying her tea. She listens to my words and the feelings behind them. She has a gentle spirit, but I think she'd be a force to deal with if someone mistreated a loved one of hers. The bottom line is, I'm developing feelings for her, and I want to let you know about this, because you're like a daughter to me."

As I listen to Poppa Pace, I realize that our relationship will have to change. I'm all right with that, because this man whom I love like a father needs a suitable companion. Sister Lovey Grace may be that companion for him. I may have to play the role of proud parent and let my Poppa Pace go to his woman. Two of his three biological children will probably rejoice at the news, but wait until his nutty daughter Tasha finds out she has even more competition for his attention. I heard she got out of the hospital a while ago and hangs out around Trenton, but I haven't seen her.

"Poppa Pace, you know I'm happy for you. I pray that Sister Grace will continue to be a blessing in your life. She seems like a faithful Christian woman, and you certainly deserve the best."

"Thank you, Daughter NikkiMac. You know, I've been praying for you and the other single Christians who desire suitable mates. I know it's sometimes a challenge for you. I'm an old man, and God has already blessed me with one wonderful wife. Many of you young single Christians haven't known that bond, and I understand that you get lonely sometimes for appropriate romantic companionship. I understand the temptations you face. That's why I pray for you. By the way, how are you and Brother Adam Greene getting along?" His question catches me by surprise. I've only talked to Jacee and Anna Maria about my one date with Adam. He's called me regularly since then, but we haven't had another date because he's involved with a major project on his job. At church, the assistant ministry keeps him busy. We chat a little when he sees me at church, but he's definitely in worship mode there, not date mode.

"Umm, things are okay with Brother Adam and me." Why am I embarrassed? I hear Poppa Pace chuckle.

"I reckon the two of us have been keeping little dating secrets from each other, huh?"

"Poppa Pace, Brother Adam keeps in touch with me, but his work schedule and church responsibilities take up a lot of his time. Actually, we've only been on one date, but I don't want to sweat him by calling him too much. I don't want him to think I'm desperate."

"Daughter NikkiMac, he asked *you* out, didn't he? As far as I know, you're the only woman he's dated in this congregation. You know lots of sisters have their eyes on him. Shoot! Even women outside the church try to get his attention! It seems to me that you're ahead of the game. You two will go out on plenty of other dates as soon as he gets his workload under control. I know you like him, because you waited this long to tell me about what's going on with you two. Don't you play too hard to get, young lady." I feel myself blush. I do like Adam, but I don't want to get my hopes up too high. Besides, I'm barely adjusting to my best friend Jacee's move. Now, my Poppa Pace has apparently found his woman, so I have to get used to Sister Lovey's space in his life. I don't need any more major adjustments. At this point, I definitely want to be realistic about Brother Adam Greene.

Chapter 19

Sister Chloe Comes Clean

My students begin to leave the Sunday school classroom while I collect pencils and clean the chalkboard. I can't help but smile, because my students' antics during the Bible memory verse activity remind me that children will be children, whether in a church classroom or a public school classroom. When Shaylonda knew her team was about to lose by a point, she coughed the correct answer to another player. When you've been teaching for a while, this student trick is easy to recognize. Of course, this meant I had to void the answer. Students always look so amazed when teachers catch them trying to be slick. Suddenly, out of the corner of my eye, I spot the figure of a woman in the classroom doorway. At first, I assume she's one of the parents, and I speak without looking up.

"Hello, the children have been dismissed. Your child is probably out in the churchyard. You know how they like to run around." No reply. I look at the doorway.

"Do you want to know why I don't like you, Sister McQuaige?" It's Sister Chloe, and she doesn't look friendly.

"Excuse me? What did you say to me?" I look around the classroom to make sure all of the children are out. It may get unpleasant in here and I don't want them to witness it.

"You know what I said. Let's sit down and have a chat." She enters the room, and for the first time, I notice her gait is off. I guess I never noticed it when we met because she was so nasty to me then that I just didn't look at her much after that. Now, I pay attention to the fact that she walks like her feet are too small, or like she has bad feet that hurt.

By the time she sits in one of the chairs, I've figured out that I can take her if I have to, but I really don't want to fight, especially not in the church building. She stares at me for a moment, and then she speaks.

"Do you know a man named Alex Carson?" My head jerks. I haven't heard from Alex in a long while, not since he was my guest here at a church service. For some time, it hurt that we parted ways, but spiritually, it was the right thing for me to do. I still miss his friendship, but realize I can't draw any more water from that well. I put on my game face and answer this woman.

"Why, yes. I know Alex, but I haven't been in contact with him for some time. Why do you ask, Sister Chloe?"

"I ask because you're the reason Alex never made a full commitment to me. He and I dated for several years. I figured he also dated other women, and that didn't worry me, but there was one that was more special than the others. That special woman turned out to be you. I know that because I bugged Alex until he told me about you. Alex says that even though he had to break contact with you, there's a place in his heart that only you can fill. I haven't given up on Alex. In fact, he and I still date each other, but he can't get you out of his head completely." She looks at me like I know what she's talking about. For a brief moment, I feel a little sorry for her. She does look hurt. However, the moment passes quickly, because this woman has been trying to give me trouble since she stepped into the church building. I begin to get hot and realize I need to pray, and soon. But first, I let a few words roll off my tongue.

"Sister Chloe, Alex and I were friends for many years. Our relationship wasn't a committed couple thing. Until I saw you in church, I didn't even know you existed. How can you blame me because you and Alex didn't seal the deal? I don't mean to be unkind, but as far as you and Alex are concerned, my name is Tess, and I ain't in this mess! I'm just about done with this weird conversation." She taps her acrylic nails on the desktop. Her nail design is intricate, full of color and shapes, like the inside of a kaleidoscope. I think it looks ghetto.

"He said you were a church woman. I had to meet you, Sister McQuaige, had to see what Alex sees in you. What do you have that I don't have?"

A light bulb clicks on in my head. "Sister Chloe, are you telling me that you became a member of this congregation just to check me out? Just because of Alex? Girl, you'd better check yourself before you wreck yourself. If I were you, I wouldn't play with God like that!" I'm beginning to think this woman has a screw loose in her head.

Unfazed, she continues. "Sister McQuaige, I plan to study you. As far as I'm concerned, my first job in this church is to make you show everybody who you really are. Then, the Christians here can see what kind of person they're dealing with. Next, I plan to show Alex who you really are so he can knock you off that pedestal in his mind." Her face looks as evil as her words sound. I shake my head, grab my purse, and prepare to leave the classroom.

"Sister Chloe, I'll pray for you."

"Knock yourself out, Sister McQuaige. Just know I've got my eyes on you." As soon as she says those words, I leave the room. I don't want to be anywhere near Sister Chloe in case God decides to react instantly to her hypocrisy and disrespect for the Lord's church. The fate of Lot's wife, in Genesis chapter 19, verse 26, comes to my mind.

Chapter 20

Lunch With Anna Maria DelGrosso

"Anna Maria, I can't believe you brought these delicious Italian stuffed mushrooms to school! You know I can't resist them! I certainly won't be getting on the scale tomorrow morning! Let me see if I can eat only one of these homemade treasures." My words don't match my actions, because both of my hands reach inside the container of stuffed mushrooms. "Mmm, these are so yummy!" Her stuffed mushrooms are one of my favorite appetizers. Anna Maria smiles.

"NikkiMac, you know I don't cook much, but my mother's Italian stuffed mushrooms recipe is one I occasionally try. I really don't think the mushrooms are that fattening, but it's hard to eat only one of them. Mine are almost as tasty as my mother's, God rest her soul. It's nice to be able to duplicate something that you learned from someone you love so much. It kind of keeps them with you. I can almost hear my mother's words instructing me as I measure, chop, stir, stuff, and bake. You know what I mean?"

"I do know, Anna Maria." I pop another stuffed mushroom into my mouth and think about my late mother, Alice McQuaige. I learned many kitchen lessons from her. I remember when she taught me how to make what she called hoecakes. Every time she said the name of this skillet-fried cornbread, I got tickled. She always said she didn't know why the bread was called hoecakes. It was what her mother called them. I can still hear my mom's soft voice instructing me.

"Nikolis, put a cup of corn meal in your mixing bowl. Mix in about a half-cup of water or milk, whichever you prefer. Use the big spoon to beat it into a smooth batter. Heat your oil, enough to cover the bottom of your frying pan, but not too much. Spoon the cornbread batter in, Baby. When you see the bubbles on the topside, it's time to turn the cornbread over so it can cook on the other side. Get a plate smaller than the skillet, but large enough to cover the cornbread. That's right, Baby. You ready to flip it? Put the plate on the bread, pick up the pan and turn it over. Hold onto the circle of bread on the plate. That's right. Now, slide the bread off the plate and back into the frying pan. Let the other side cook now. When you see the edges get crisp, it's time to use the spatula and get it out of the pan. It should look sort of like a yellow pancake, with a few brown spots. Wonderful, Nikolis, you did a fine job! It looks and smells great! Let's taste it!"

I return from my mother's presence in my head and recognize Anna Maria's blue eyes staring at me. "Hey, where'd you go just then, NikkiMac? You seemed miles away. Were you in a sad place in your mind?" Anna Maria's eyes are full of concern.

"I'm okay, Anna Maria. What you said made me think about one of the precious times I spent in the kitchen with my mother. I was thinking about how she taught me to make skillet-fried cornbread."

"NikkiMac, that's something else we have in common. Both of our wonderful mothers have crossed over to the other side. We'll always miss them. I know your father has crossed over too, but Mr. Pace has stepped into a fatherly role for you. Has anyone become motherly for you?"

"No, Anna Maria, but I do appreciate my Poppa Pace. He's a blessing, he really is. Tell me about your father. Is he still alive?"

"Yes, my father lives in a senior housing development in Ewing Township. For a couple of years after my mother passed, he lived alone in their home, but then decided he wanted to be around more people his own age. He loves the place he moved into, and there are lots of activities. Also, he doesn't have to worry about maintaining a property. There's an onsite cleaning service and medical facility. I see him several times a week. In fact, I have to make sure I call him first, because his social calendar is so full. As long as he's happy, I'm happy for him to be there. He cracks me up, because he walks around there and croons and woos the senior ladies like he's Frank Sinatra or Dean Martin!" We share a hearty laugh.

"Anna Maria, a while ago, you told me you had a singing career right after high school. What happened with that?"

Her eyebrows crease and a storm forms in her eyes "It's not easy to talk about, NikkiMac. I let myself get played for a fool by a con artist named Ben Bailey. He posed as a successful talent agent. My dear Mama DelGrosso distrusted this man from the start, but I didn't listen to her. I wanted to be a star, and he swore he could make it happen." Anna Maria tosses her full head of hair and narrows her lips.

"Don't beat yourself up, Anna Maria. You were young and naïve." I gently pat her shoulder and encourage her to continue.

"I was an okay student at Trenton High School, but I could've done better academically. To be honest with you, I was more interested in music than academic or business subjects. As long as I got a B or C grade in non-music studies, I was satisfied. Music has always made me feel alive, NikkiMac, and I was great at singing. I started performing solos in the tenth grade, and by the time I was a senior, I'd performed at community and church events all over Trenton. I started to believe the hype. I thought I could pass over all the other talented high school vocalists and go straight to the music industry and to Broadway. I thought I didn't have to pay my dues or gradually work my way to the top. My head got big from listening to people tell me I was the best soprano to ever come through Trenton High School. I didn't see the need for a college degree, because in my mind, I was destined for success in the music industry."

Anna Maria pauses and looks at her polished candy apple red fingernails. She appears wistful and somewhat wounded. I'm eager to hear the rest of her story, but I keep quiet.

"At Trenton High School, I was trained by the greatest vocal music teacher ever, Mr. Redlum. I'll always be thankful to him for the fantastic range of music he taught us: classical, opera, jazz, Broadway show tunes, and more. We learned so much about music from him. He was the best. Anyway, news about my voice spread. Some people told me about an agent who was asking about me. After I sang at a benefit concert organized by the Sisters with Attitude book club, I met Ben Bailey. He introduced himself to me and laid out his vision for taking me to the top in the music industry. Later on, my school counselor, my teachers, my parents, and even members of Sisters with Attitude cautioned me against Ben's words, but I was hardheaded. I made the wrong decision. Of course, it didn't help that Ben Bailey was in my ear, telling me I should grab fame and fortune right away. He claimed it was my time, and I should go for it. I believed him, with all his flash and dash." Her voice trails off.

"What did he do to you, Anna Maria?" I ask softly.

"He made false promises and took my money, NikkiMac. He convinced me to sign papers and keep our plans secret. He helped me keep my parents off our trail by providing them with applications for music training schools that he found for me. My parents didn't trust him, but they knew little about this process. Ben supposedly booked me at important singing engagements in New York that were to begin in July, soon after my high school graduation. This kept me excited about how hard he was working on my singing career. By the time I paid his fee with most of the money my folks had saved to help me with my first year of music training school or college, Ben Bailey had left Trenton and taken my money with him."

Anna Maria's drooped shoulders and downcast eyes make me comprehend the depth of her embarrassment. I'm stunned by her revelation, and I wonder how she could have allowed herself to be tricked like that, but I try not to show it. I can tell that Anna Maria feels bad enough about her mistake. She doesn't need me to rub her nose in it. I sit in silence, and she continues.

"NikkiMac, you probably wonder what happened to Ben Bailey. Let me just say this: I have some mighty protective uncles here in New Jersey and also in New York. I lost time in getting my education, but I got my money back. I learned a life lesson as well. Furthermore, Ben Bailey learned not to mess with the DelGrosso family." Anna Maria ends this sentence with a defiant stare into space. Her blue eyes ice over and her posture straightens. I can relate to what she's saying. It makes me feel relieved that I'm counted as her friend and not as her enemy.

"Anna Maria, say no more. We all make mistakes. By the way, I've got some protective cousins in the Carolinas that know how to handle their business, much like your uncles." We both laugh. I place my last stuffed mushroom on a napkin and give her a hug. Just then, the bell rings. Our school lunch break is over.

Chapter 21

Remembrances, Goodbyes, Mistakes

Anna Maria and I are near the cemetery in Ewing Township. We drive past the shopping center and public library on our left before we turn right and enter through the cemetery's open wrought iron gates. Out of respect for the deceased, the two of us end our chatter. My two parents and Anna Maria's mother are buried here. Nickson and Alice McQuaige are buried side by side in an area near the cemetery office. Anna Maria's mother, Lucia, is buried nearby. Anna Maria and I discovered this when we once saw each other carrying flowers for our parents' gravesites. I park my car near the small office building and we get out to walk. At the fork in the road that leads to the gravesites, Anna Maria walks to the left while I walk in the opposite direction. I listen as I tap my crackly bag of clear blue glass stones against my thigh and count tombstones to the row where my parents' remains rest. Once I recognize the end gravestone I use as my marker, I walk down the row to the double McQuaige gravestone. No matter how many times I take this walk, it still feels disrespectful to walk over the graves of others in order to get to my parents'. There's no other way, though, because it's not like it used to be. There are so many more graves here than when my parents were placed in the ground. Here they are. I kneel and trace the carved letters of their names on their tombstones. Next, I trace the birth and death dates of my parents. The stones feel cool and smooth underneath my fingers.

"Hey, Mommy and Daddy. I know you're not really here. I know it's just your remains here and that your spirits went back to God who gave them to you. You're in my thoughts every day, even though you've been away from me for so many years. Look! I brought your blue glass stones to make your spot look pretty. When the sun hits them, they really sparkle!" I place the smooth glass stones in a neat line so that they decorate the small ledge at the base of headstone. Some blue stones are still here from my last visit, although the rain has moved them out of line formation. I return them to order, and dust off the headstones. I give myself permission to shed a few fat tears. The wet tears leave cool tracks as they roll down my freckled cheeks and fall off my chin.

"See you later, Mommy and Daddy McQuaige. I miss you so much and love you forever." A few minutes later, Anna Maria and I meet by my car, where we hug like long lost sisters.

"You okay, NikkiMac?"

"Yes, I'll be all right in a minute. How about you, Anna Maria?"

"Same here. God surely blessed both of us with wonderful parents, huh?"

"Amen to that, Anna Maria. Amen to that. Well, I guess it's time for me to drop you off at home." It's quiet in the car as we travel the winding road toward the cemetery's wrought iron gates. We leave this place, but we have our memories.

After I drop Anna Maria off at her West Trenton home, I take Route 29 south to drive back in the direction of downtown Trenton. The Delaware River is a little high, but thankfully, we haven't had any flooding this year. A few joggers are visible on the foot and bike path. Near the shaky bridge, an outdoor exercise class moves in catlike motion. The exit ramp near the War Memorial Building is not busy on this Saturday morning, so I sail through the light and go by the memorial and make a left onto John Fitch Way. Too late, I remember the irritating traffic light at John Fitch Way and South Warren Street. This traffic light takes forever to turn green. It seems to go through three or four cycles before the green light appears. I don't know who's responsible for this, but I'd like them to be forced to travel this route on a regular basis. That way, they'd be as annoyed with this traffic light as I am. Since I start out on Route 29, it should be faster to get from West Trenton to East Trenton. It often takes less time to drive through downtown, with its stop and go traffic and jaywalkers, than to drive the highway, because this light eats up so much time.

I grumble out loud. "I hate it when I forget and drive this way! Why do we have to drive all around buck yard's bend to get from one spot to the other! Only in Trenton!"

By the time I get a few blocks past the police station on North Clinton Avenue, I see something disturbing and strange. It's Cletus, and he's staggering like the drunk he once was. I beep my car horn and pull over to the curb near him. "Cletus! Cletus!" I yell as I get out of my car. I wave at him in a further effort to get his attention. I get close enough to see that he looks raggedy, and his eyes are bloodshot. He stops and looks at me as plain as day, then turns the nearest corner and ducks into an alley. Without hesitation, I run right behind him. Drunk or not, this former high school track star is still faster than I am. I can't run and holler at the same time, so I just run. The only sounds are the rustle of bushes that line the narrow alley, our pounding footsteps, and our heavy breathing. We're about to run out of alley, so I suck in a big gob of air, lengthen my stride, and pump my arms to get more speed. About ten seconds later, my feet trip over a discarded bicycle handlebar, and down I go.

"Aieee! Ow! Ow! Ow! My ankle!" My right ankle hurts like several yellow jacket wasps just stung it. I gingerly twist my body so I can get on my knees, grab a bush for support, and stand up. That's when I feel strong hands catch me under my arms and lift me to my feet.

"NikkiMac, you ought to know better than to follow me down an alley. I've been running through these East Trenton alleys most of my life. I know them like I know the back of my hand." Cletus brushes the dirt and leaves from my clothes, and I see tears in his eyes. "Your ankle okay? Can you put weight on it?" I smell the liquor on his breath and sense that his spirit is broken. At first, he avoids eye contact and busies himself with dusting me off.

"Cletus, I'm okay, I think I just twisted it a little. If you help me, I can limp back to my car. Why in the world did you run from me?" I grab his hands and hold them.

"NikkiMac, I ran because I didn't want you to see that I've been drinking today." He looks down at his hands but he doesn't take them away from mine.

"Cletus, what happened? You've been doing so well all these months, attending your AA meetings, coming to church, spending time with and planning a future with Angeleese and the children . . ."

"My mother died this morning, NikkiMac." I want to open my mouth and say something, but I need to process his words. Oddly, I consider that while Anna Maria and I were honoring our departed parents at the cemetery this morning, Cletus' mother was involved with the business of dying.

"Oh Cletus, I'm so sorry! Why didn't you call Brother Pace, or me? Wait a minute; aren't you supposed to first call your alcohol counselor or sponsor, someone like that? You didn't have to have a drink!" Cletus fixes his gaze on me for quite a while before he responds, and this makes me uncomfortable. Finally, he speaks.

"NikkiMac, I did call someone. I called Mr. Alcohol, because this morning, I helped the funeral director carry my mother's body in a zipped-up tarp from her bed to his car. I felt like God had turned His face away from me. Why did God do this to me? Since I've been in the church, I've tried to do right. I stopped drinking alcohol. I go to church every Sunday. I attend the group meetings to help keep me strong against alcohol. I take care of my mother. I try to do right by my twins and Angeleese, as well as her other children. I helped Angeleese get baptized. I think about marrying her. I spend time with a strong Christian like Brother Foster Pace and other faithful Christians like you. But all that wasn't enough, because God still took my mother." Cletus looks more than drunk; he looks defeated.

At first, I don't know what to say to him. I don't want to say the wrong thing, so I remain silent for a minute. Then, I reach out and hug him. He responds by wrapping one arm around me so he can help me walk, and we leave the alley together. I finally figure out what to say. "Cletus, please believe that God still loves you. I know He'll help you get through this. Right now, you're coming home with me to eat and then sleep this off. We'll call Brother Pace and your sponsor. They'll help us figure out what to do next."

Chapter 22

Lucy Bergamot's Place

"NikkiMac, isn't that the place where you get your hair done?" Anna Maria questions me as we drive by Lucy's Bergamot's House of Style and Beauty. Lucy's place is a few blocks from the church building, where Anna Maria and I worked a few hours earlier this morning with the monthly feeding program. Jacee and I used to do this together before she left for her graduate program. I miss her, but we keep in touch by phone, text, and online. However, it's not the same as being with her, since Jacee and I have been together for so long. I support her plan to earn her Masters Degree, though. I also plan to pursue my next degree also. In the meantime, I'm thankful to have Anna Maria as a friend. This situation makes me think of the saying, "When God closes one door, He opens another."

Recently, after hearing the announcements about our monthly feeding program, Anna Maria did something that surprised me. She approached our minister after a Sunday morning service. "Brother Johnson, I know I'm not a member of this congregation, but I'd really like to help with the monthly feeding program here. It would mean a lot for me to be a part of a good cause like this one. May I do that?" Brother Johnson thought for a second, then smiled at Anna Maria and shook her hand before he replied.

"Miss Anna Maria, we'd be happy to have you aboard. I'll speak to Brother Pace and let him know you'll be joining us as a volunteer. Sister NikkiMac will give you the details. Right, Sister NikkiMac?"

"Of course, Brother Johnson." I turned to Anna Maria and teased, "You sure don't waste any time getting involved, do you?" I was quite pleased about her desire to become more involved with the church.

She ignored my joking tone and responded, "Not when I know something is the right thing to do and I'm able to do it, NikkiMac." I remember her look of determination and sincerity that day. Anna Maria has volunteered in the program ever since.

My thoughts return to the present, and to Anna Maria's question about the hair salon. "Yes, Anna Maria. Miss Lucy's is the place I go to for my perms, hair care products and hair care advice. She's a character, and she'll fuss you out, but she truly knows how to keep hair healthy and good-looking. It's even more than that; each client is special to her. Whether she praises or scolds them, she makes her clients feel important, listened to, and cared about. On top of that, she does all types of hair, from nappy to straight. She even has some male clients who get haircuts and shampoos from her. She does a lot of good work in the community. As a matter of fact, we do have some time to stop in the shop. I want to you to meet her."

"Sounds good to me!" I drive into the salon's parking lot. A neon sign flashes: *Lucy Bergamot's House of Style and Beauty. Referrals from current clients are necessary for appointments.* When Anna Maria reads the last part of the sign, she raises her perfect eyebrows. We walk into the shop and observe the small, tastefully decorated waiting room to the left. The chairs look comfortable. Current issues of magazines and newspapers rest neatly on a mahogany coffee table. Books stand in order on two mahogany bookshelves. In the room to the right are six operator chairs, four with hairdryers attached. The opposite side of the long room has three sinks. The far wall is mostly lined with hair products and there's a mirrored nook. Here, clients can see their hair from all angles, but only after Miss Lucy has completed her hair magic. I found out the hard way that I should wait until Miss Lucy is finished before I touch my hair or reach for a mirror. The snap of her small-toothed black plastic comb against the back of my exploring hand is a memory not yet erased.

Right now, Miss Lucy is all cranked up while she delivers one of her famous lectures to a misbehaving client. The patterns on her short-sleeved dress come to life as she gestures with her arms in between moving her hands through her client's hair. This is the way she stresses her points. I lead Anna Maria off to the side and out of the line of verbal fire. We watch as Miss Lucy's quick hands use a wide-toothed comb to part the client's hair into four sections. Her hands twist and clamp these sections. Then, she returns to the first section, unravels it, and smoothes a white creamy straightening product onto the client's new hair growth, starting at the roots. The scent of ammonia floats across the room. She sets the timer for Portia's hair.

"Miss Portia, I've told you a thousand times about waiting so long to have your perm retouched. I know how you love to scratch your scalp, and I hope you told me the truth when you said you didn't scratch it. You aren't allowed to scratch your scalp before any chemical is put in your hair. We'll find out about that very soon, won't we?" Portia shakes her head from side to side and wisely keeps her mouth closed. She manages to fix a contrite expression on her face. In another part of the room, a young lady we call Fancy laughs softly at Portia. This is not lost on Miss Lucy. She tosses her long dreadlocks back over her shoulders. The sun shines through a shop window and highlights Miss Lucy's face. Her skin color reminds me of expensive dark caramel candy.

"I really don't know what you're sniggling and giggling about, Miss Fancy! Take that acrylic skullcap off your head. Look at your hair. It's as dry as dust. I keep telling you that your natural hair needs to breathe and it also needs to be moisturized! Instead of ducking me when it's time for your deep conditioning treatments and slapping those cheap dollar store caps on your head, you ought to be right here in this chair. You need to try and save your damaged hair. All that money you spend on all those different caps could pay for your hair treatments!"

Fancy's laughter ends. Miss Lucy completes Portia's perm application, peels off her plastic gloves, and tosses them in the disposal can. Then, she puts a clear plastic cap on Portia and lets the elastic snap. Portia's head jerks a little, but she remains silent. Miss Lucy sets the timer and motions for Portia to sit out in one of the other chairs. Next, Miss Lucy surveys the room. I don't think she's finished with her diatribe. Fancy is next, but she doesn't move to Miss Lucy's chair right away. "That's all right, I can't tell you people a thing. What do I know?" She gestures with her shoulders hunched up and her palms facing the ceiling. Then, she places her hands on her curvy hips and states, "Oh, that's right! I'm the only hair care *expert* in this room! I guess some of you don't pay any attention to my degree and training certificates that are on prominent display on these walls." She waves her arms in a sweeping gesture and points out her documents of achievement. "Well, I can't make you all act right, but please give me credit for trying to take the best care of my customers' hair that I can! No matter how much I fuss, you know I love you enough to tell you what you need to know."

Nobody says a word, because to do so will make Lucy go off for another ten minutes. Shortly, the storm appears to be over. Miss Lucy takes a deep breath and a calm comes over her attractive face. She gazes at Anna Maria, then at me. She smiles and shows off the cute dimples in her cheeks. "Miss NikkiMac, what's up, Baby? And who's your pretty Italian friend?"

Anna Maria approaches Miss Lucy with confidence. "I'm Anna Maria DelGrosso. It's a pleasure to meet you, Miss Lucy. Yes, I'm Italian, but how did you know that before you heard my last name?"

Miss Lucy Bergamot pauses before she flashes her biggest smile, the one that says, "I truly know who I am and it's all good with me." Her large eyes with their jet-black pupils seem to have little sparkles in them. "Child, Miss Lucy Bergamot knows a lot of things. At first I thought you were mixed with African American or Latino and Caucasian, but that's not it. You see, back in the day, I lived in a Trenton neighborhood near the Italian section called Chambersburg, so I recognize the look. For a minute, your bright blue eyes threw me off, but one of my Italian friends has blue-eyed relatives from the north part of Italy. I'm very pleased to meet you. Any friend of NikkiMac's is welcome in my world."

"Thanks, Miss Lucy." Anna Maria stares with innocent curiosity at Miss Lucy's latest personal hairstyle: thick dreadlocks that are bleached blond at the ends, but are black about five inches closer to the roots. Before I can signal Anna Maria to change her face, Miss Lucy catches Anna Maria's expression.

"You like?" Her eyes twinkle as she shows her brilliant white-toothed smile to all in the room. She doesn't wait for Anna Maria's response. "Well, I woke up one day and decided to see if blondes really do have extra fun. So, I made myself a blonde. I got bored with it after awhile, so I'm letting it grow out. It turns out I have fun no matter what color my hair is, and my hair has been many colors!" Miss Lucy laughs softly. She's such an exotic creature, all curves and bright colors.

With her usual candor, Anna Maria replies, "You could just wear different-colored wigs instead of bleaching or dyeing your natural hair. It seems that would do less damage." The salon gets quiet. I want to snap my fingers and make my friend disappear so we can get out of the way of Miss Lucy's coming rant.

Miss Lucy's laughter comes to an abrupt halt. "Are you trying to be smart with me, DelGrosso?" Out of the corner of my eye, I see a customer slip into the other room. Fancy and Portia put their magazines up close to their faces. I pray silently. Anna Maria looks like she's almost figured out that her usual forthrightness is unwelcome here. Just then, the timer sounds off for Portia's hair.

"Ding!" The timer signals to Miss Lucy, and she reaches over to shut it off. Then, Miss Lucy looks at Anna Maria for a second before she speaks to Portia. "How does your scalp feel? Is it burning any?"

"It's just about to, Miss Lucy."

"Okay, go over to the sink so I can rinse you, Portia."

I grab Anna Maria by the arm and move toward the door with her while announcing, "Miss Lucy, I'll call you later this week to schedule a relaxer, and maybe some color. Okay?"

"NikkiMac, how many times do I have to tell you? When you double the chemicals, you double the damage. You know I won't do a relaxer and a color treatment on the same visit! Sometimes I just don't know what to do with these unruly clients of mine!" She gives me one of her motherly smiles, like I'm the idiot in the village, but she loves me anyway. She stares at Anna Maria. "Oh, Miss DelGrosso, we'll talk again. Yes, we will. Ciao, dear." Miss Lucy places her hands on her hips and her smile has a little warning in it. In words, the warning goes like this: *You don't know me like that, Missy Anna, but we'll be just fine before long.* Sooner than Anna Maria can form a response, I rush her out of Lucy Bergamot's House of Style and Beauty.

Chapter 23

That Young Preacher

Worship service starts in another five minutes. I'm in my usual pew, and I think about Jacee. I spoke with her last night, and her studies are going well. A couple of minutes later, Anna Maria sits next to me and kisses both sides of my face. I've come to understand that this is her thing. She says everyone in her family greets this way. It's kind of fun, so I go along with it.

"Happy Sunday, NikkiMac. Isn't one of the young men from Brother Johnson's preacher training class scheduled to speak this morning?"

"Yes, but I don't know which one. Hmm, I notice that you keep up with the events here like you're a member. Why don't you make that move and get baptized into the church? You agree that what the Bible says is the truth."

Anna Maria bats those exquisite long eyelashes of hers and enunciates each syllable as she blinks rapidly. "NikkiMac, it's not that I haven't thought about it. I want to learn more, and that's why I attend worship services here so regularly. My father even asked me about it. He knows I haven't attended a worship service with him in years, and he notices my interest in what's going on here. I really learn so much by reading along in the Bible and having the scriptures made clear." Before I can reply, Brother Sampson walks up front to lead the opening prayer.

"NikkiMac, isn't that the police officer who helped you when you thought you had an intruder in your house? Is he married?" Anna Maria whispers.

"Why do you want to know, Missy?" I raise one eyebrow and wink at her. Then, I bow my head for prayer. Following prayer, Brother Vincent comes forward to lead songs. We sing *Did You Think To Pray?* and *Where Could I Go?* Then, it's time for communion. Five brothers walk to the wooden communion table and stand shoulder to shoulder behind it. They face the congregation, and one brother speaks.

"It's time for us to note the death, burial, and resurrection of our Lord and Savior Jesus Christ. He died for the forgiveness of our sins. Our example is found in First Corinthians chapter 11, verses 23 through 32." The brother reads the verses out loud and we follow along in our Bibles. "Brother Carlos, please pray for the bread."

"Heavenly Father, please bless this bread, which represents the body of Christ. Let us partake of it with clean hands and pure hearts. Amen."

The lead brother says, "Brother Sampson, please pray for the fruit of the vine."

"Let's bow our heads. Our Father in heaven, Your name is holy. Please bless the fruit of the vine, which represents the blood of Christ that was shed for us." Each of the five brothers at the table takes communion before they move out to distribute it to the congregation. After communion, we sing two more songs before Minister Johnson goes to the podium to make an announcement.

"Church, our young Brother Scott Harvin will soon come before us with the gospel message for today. My heart is glad, because Brother Scott regularly attends my Saturday morning preacher training class. He has shown so much progress. This eighteen year-old has become one of my sons in the gospel. Please hear him!"

Brother Scott Harvin walks to the podium and shows a shy smile. I observe some of the older teen girls, and even younger Shaylonda, sit up and take notice. She's doing well since the situation with her mother's former hairdresser was addressed. Brother Sampson made sure justice was done. Iris and I made sure Shaylonda received the counseling she needed.

Brother Scott Harvin clears his throat and then begins. "Thank you, Brother Johnson. I appreciate you for allowing me to speak to the congregation today. I want to talk briefly about what the world calls self-sufficiency. To the faithful Christian, this concept is a fallacy, because we know that we're totally dependent on God through Jesus

Christ. Please travel with me to Matthew chapter 11, verses 25 through 30. The words of Jesus are recorded here. In verse 27, Jesus tells us that He completely *knows* God. Let's read together about the intimate, unique, and personal knowledge of God that is gained through Jesus." There's the sound of Bible pages turning, and then the congregation reads the passage out loud together.

"Yes! I love to hear us read the Bible together, my brothers and sisters. Check this out. At the end of this passage, Jesus lets us know that we can put down our heavy yokes, or our burdens. He tells us how we can have rest for our souls. You know, we try to earn rest for our souls with our efforts, checklists, and opinions. We sometimes put tradition before doctrine in order to *earn* rest for our souls. We can't earn rest for our souls because it's a *gift* from Jesus Christ. However, we can exchange our oppressive yokes for the easy yoke of Jesus. Here's an added bonus: Jesus knows each one of us so well that He provides us *custom-fitted yokes*, y'all! What can be better than that?"

"Amen, young brother!"

"Thank you, Jesus!"

"Glory!"

Brother Harvin mops his brow with a handkerchief and exclaims, "Help me, Lord!"

"Preach it, young man!" shouts Brother Johnson.

"When you come to our Lord and Savior Jesus Christ, He gets beside you and helps you carry your burden. What a blessing!"

"Hallelujah!"

"Amen!"

"That's right, Brother Harvin!"

"So, if you're a member of the body of Christ, but you haven't fully given Jesus your old yoke and your heart, now is the time to make this right. If you haven't yet come to Jesus, because you're trying to earn your salvation, why not come to Jesus today?"

After a few more points about how to get into the right relationship with God, young Brother Scott Harvin gives the invitation once more, and Brother Vincent leads us in *Jesus Will Give You Rest*. Two people come forward to be baptized into the body of Christ. Our minister, Brother Johnson, takes their confessions and they're escorted to the dressing rooms to change into the clothes for baptism. Brother Johnson's face is radiant as he walks over to Brother Harvin, shakes his hand, and puts his arm around the young man's shoulder.

"Church, as you can see, God has blessed our young Brother Scott Harvin with the gift of preaching."

"Amen!"

"Yes sir, brother!"

"I know that's right!"

Brother Johnson continues, "This is why nobody can tell me it's a waste of time to teach interested young men about ministering the gospel. A church could have a budding preacher in their midst, but never know it, because no one took the time to cultivate this dream in a young man's mind. We have to be careful not to quench the Spirit in our young people. Besides, our young men face many temptations. We should rejoice when they choose to learn about the Bible. Am I right about it?"

"Amen, Brother Johnson!"

"That's right!"

Our minister looks at Brother Scott Harvin the way a proud father looks at his son. Young Brother Scott looks humble and happy. One person is baptized and then the other. We sing *There Is A Fountain* as each one rises from the water in the baptism pool. They return to the dressing rooms to change back into their clothing while service continues with the collection of the offering. After prayer for the offering, Brother Flowers begins the announcements.

"We thank our young Brother Scott Harvin for the wonderful message he preached this morning. We give thanks for the two souls who came forward for baptism and are now members of the body of Christ."

"Praise the Lord!"

"Amen, brother."

"When our new members come from the dressing rooms, I'll introduce them to the congregation. Before you leave, please take a moment and give our new members the right hand of fellowship. Greet them and let them know you're excited they're part of the body. Encourage them and make them feel like family, because they are."

"NikkiMac, I'm going make sure to greet the new members," whispers Anna Maria. She wears a purposeful expression.

"How're you going to welcome someone to a group that you're not officially a part of?" I smile at her, but I mean what I say. Anna Maria blinks a few times, returns my smile, and remains silent.

However, her face says, "You're not the boss of me, NikkiMac." I love it.

Chapter 24

At The Gym

A while ago, Anna Maria told me about a gym located in Ewing Township, not far away from the Trenton city limits. Although I protested that my tight schedule didn't allow for an exercise class, Anna Maria was relentless.

"NikkiMac, I went to Lucy Bergamot's place with you, so you have to come to my gym with me. Check it out; I'm sure you'll like it. Besides, this circuit-training workout only takes thirty minutes. I work out three times a week and in only a few months, I've already lost five pounds and three inches! I have a guest pass and you're coming with me after school this Thursday, so bring your workout gear. We can change after school and go to the gym. Don't worry; you don't have to look cute. The gym is for women only." I went to the gym with her that Thursday, and I was sold.

Now that I'm a member of the gym, I squeeze in three sessions a week. It's best for me to come right after I leave school on Tuesdays, Thursdays, and Fridays. I'd love to work out on Mondays, but that's when our school principal holds the weekly staff meetings. The meetings go on so long that I'm too brain dead to even think about the gym before I go home. Sometimes I think educators spend more time talking about what needs to be done than actually doing what needs to be done. Although, for a time, I did work with a principal who rolled up her sleeves and climbed down into the trenches right along with her staff in order to meet the needs of the students. She was a firecracker with exciting ideas. Unfortunately, she was snatched up by the administration and ushered into an assistant superintendent position. When she realized her skills worked better within the school setting, she transferred to another school in the district because our principal slot had been filled in her absence. Maybe she'll be able to get back to our school one day. It's hard to get situated on a good team.

That's why I enjoy this gym. The owner, circuit coaches, and the members work well together. We're a group of women of many different races and ages, but we encourage one another to gain and maintain good health.

I drive into the parking lot this afternoon, and spot feisty Josephine as she exits the gym. She unties her bandana headband from her short brunette haircut and waves it in my direction. "Hey, Miss Josephine. You beat me here today, I see."

"Hello, NikkiMac. Yeah, I took off a half-day from work because of my dental appointment. I figured I might as well do my workout before sitting in the dentist's chair. The workout takes care of my aggression. I'm less likely to hit the dentist for giving me a needle!"

"Ha! I know that's right. See you next time."

"Oh, Pat wants to know if you're free for dinner one night next week, NikkiMac. She already spoke to Therese and Jean. The five of us are overdue for our monthly Girls' Night at our favorite pizza place. I feel the need for a real tomato pie and that delicious antipasto!"

"Looking forward to it, Josephine. I'm sure Pat will email me soon, because she's serious about being our group's organizer." We share a laugh before Josephine walks to her car and I enter the gym. Once inside, I see Bella, a quiet, unpretentious woman who works for the state of New Jersey. Her office building is nearby, and I think she lives in Ewing Township. Bella always looks like she's thinking about something. When I first met her, I thought she was aloof, but now I understand she's merely quiet until someone engages her in conversation. We discuss books and we share recipes. It turns out that she and I both grew up in Trenton, but at different times. We also lived in different neighborhoods, and her parents settled in Trenton long before mine did. Bella and I like to compare notes about life in Trenton back in the day. In fact, several of the ladies at the gym are older, and they remember downtown Trenton as a grand place back in the 1960's and earlier.

I hear Pepper's shriek of delight as I sign in at the desk. She holds a small blue gift bag, and I remember that we talked last month about her hobby. She knits one-of-a-kind socks. "NikkiMac, do I have a surprise for you!" Her wide smile shows off her dimples. She waves the little blue bag with so much enthusiasm that Mary, the circuit coach, stops entering data on the computer.

"What are you two girls up to? Are you starting trouble, Pepper?"

"Well, of course I am! It's what I do!" Pepper's gray eyes twinkle with mischief.

"What's in the bag, Pepper?" I ask.

"I brought two of my most colorful handmade socks for you to see. You told me you like socks, and I thought of you when I knitted them. They're made of good, durable 70 percent wool and a 30 percent specialty sock yarn, so there's a little give in them. You said you wear a size 8 shoe, like me, so I made these using my foot measurement. I made the heel wider than the average manufactured socks. I used the perfect sized needles and made the socks pop with color, because you told me you like colors in your socks. Wait until you see my special surprise feature. NikkiMac, you and I have a ball laughing and teasing one another while we work out, and you're also a great listener. These are for you." She reaches into the bag, pulls out two brilliantly colored socks, and hands them to me.

"Pepper, they're gorgeous! I've never seen socks quite like these before. Check out the tiny pocket on each sock. Keys or a small cell phone can fit in here! That's your special feature! These are perfectly knitted and their thickness is just right! Thank you so very much." As I give her a hug of appreciation, it dawns on me that Pepper has a spicy name and a hard shell, but a mild and sometimes tender center.

"You're welcome, NikkiMac. I know you've invited me to church a few times, and I haven't accepted your invitation. I'm not much into church these days, but I appreciate your spirit. Don't stop inviting me, though. I just might surprise you one of these days. In the meantime, enjoy your socks." We give each other a high five. Three or four of the other women walk over to examine the socks. Each one of them raves about the uniqueness and the quality of Pepper's sock creations.

"I see you used different stitches in the heel and ankle area. Nice!"

"Well done. It looks like you used two different needle sizes, Pepper. Very intricate."

"How long did it take to make them?"

"I want a pair of Pepper socks, too!"

Pepper laughs at the last remark and answers the rest of the ladies' questions. Mary, our friendly circuit coach, intends for us to get our best workouts. She steps into our conversation. "Okay ladies, let's get back to your workouts. You can talk about the lovely socks while you exercise. I want you to keep your cardio rates up in between working the machines."

Brenda watches all the action while she continues on the circuit. Now, she manages to remark, "Hey, Pepper, those are really special. How long did it take you to make them?" Brenda often asks questions after they've already been answered. I think it's because she tries to keep up with every conversation on the circuit. We tease her about this, but she doesn't mind. I try to stay a few machines ahead of her on the circuit, because her conversations slow her down and hold up my progress. She knows when I do this. She calls me on it and chuckles about it, but her behavior remains the same. It's all good.

These are some nice ladies, and the interesting thing is that many of us probably wouldn't hang out together in any other setting. Here, we have the same purpose and we feel comfortable interacting closely with ladies from different circles. As far as race is concerned, it's like the United Nations in here. Many of the ladies live in Ewing, some live in Trenton, and others work in the area but live in neighboring cities. For several women, it's convenient to work out here at lunchtime or after work before their commute home. Mary and I often remark that people from various cultures are more the same than they are different. Several relationships have extended beyond the gym. Some of us choose to spend time with each other at restaurants, on trips, and in other places. That's what happened with Josephine, Therese, Jean, Pat, and me.

Pepper completes her workout and calls out, "See you later, ladies." Several ladies call out their goodbyes and best wishes for a good remainder of the day. It's a sociable crowd. A few minutes later, Saraah and Margaret enter.

Brenda says, "I'm glad you're here, Saraah. Now we can get the answer to the daily word puzzle. Hurry up and look at the board. I know you can help us solve this one."

"Hello, ladies. I'm later than usual because I had a medical appointment this morning. Let me see," Saraah responds. Within thirty seconds, she rattles off an answer. She's correct, as usual. We all marvel at how she figures these out so fast.

"I told you Saraah would get the answer!" Brenda sounds so proud one would think she'd discovered the answer herself.

"I keep telling you that I work on puzzles at home while I have my coffee. You know I retired long ago, so I use puzzles, reading, and travel to help keep my mind sharp. It's all about enjoying life." Her bright smile sparkles.

Margaret steps onto a recovery pad near me. "NikkiMac and Helen, last night I cooked the roasted turkey legs that I told you both about. Girls, they were so tender that the meat fell off the bones! NikkiMac, you should pick some up while they're on sale at Shop Rite this week."

"I have some in the freezer, Margaret. I'll defrost them tomorrow and cook them." The thought of tender and juicy roasted turkey legs makes me hungry.

"NikkiMac, don't forget to put about an inch of water in the pan before you put them in the oven. Cover them tightly with foil, and put the hot sauce on them in the last thirty minutes of cooking. You can brown them if you want the top layer to be crispy. Just take the foil off and roast them for another ten minutes, uncovered."

Helen laughs. "NikkiMac, don't forget to bring me one of those turkey legs. Why is it that within the first few minutes of exercise, we begin to talk about food?"

Mary answers, "Because we're great cooks, and we enjoy eating what we cook. That's also why we have to work out!" Then, she turns up the music to inspire us to move our bodies more and our mouths less. This works for me, and I step up my pace. After two more times around the circuit, my body feels great and my program is complete.

While I do my cool down stretches in the rear of the gym, Della enters. I know it's her before I see her, because her distinctive voice rolls from the front door to the back of the room. She's on the circuit before quick, flashing her striking, large round eyes and snapping her well-manicured fingers to the beat. Della's cherry colored lips highlight her radiant smile.

"All right now! This music is nice, Mary! Makes me want to move!" That's Della, the queen of sassy and classy.

Chapter 25

Welcome Home

"I'm glad you were home when I called, Daughter NikkiMac. Thanks for letting me stop by. I've got a surprise for you." As Poppa Pace smiles at me, his eyes twinkle with joy. He enters my home, then turns around and waves to someone sitting in his parked car.

"Who's that in your car? Why don't you ask them to come inside?" I'm curious, but not overly concerned, because Poppa Pace often helps out by giving someone a ride. He's full of good deeds. I surely remember how he first came to my assistance long ago.

"That's okay, NikkiMac, he can wait in the car. I'll just be here a few minutes." He eases himself into my recliner and takes a deep breath. I notice the gray curly hair in his sideburns and in his heavy eyebrows.

"Two things, Daughter NikkiMac. First, I plan to ask Sister Lovey Grace to be my wife, and I hope she'll accept my proposal of marriage."

"God bless the two of you, Poppa Pace. Don't worry about me trying to get in the way, because I know a wife has first place. Sister Lovey is a wonderful lady, and I can tell she makes you happy."

"Daughter NikkiMac, what you just said means so much to me. You'll always have a place in my heart. There's a second thing I want you to know. An old friend has been away from you and has now returned. He's eager to be reacquainted with you and he asked me to help him out." My head spins. Is it Alex Carson? Has he decided to accept the gospel? Maybe Poppa Pace did a better job than I did with teaching him about the Bible. Is it one of the men I knew from my bar days? If it is, I hope he wasn't too graphic in describing some of my club outfits. That would be embarrassing.

"Daughter NikkiMac, I'll signal him to come inside. Turn around, so you can truly be surprised." I do as I'm told. Soon, I hear the screen door close and footsteps in my living room.

"Okay, you can turn around now." I turn slowly, with my eyes closed. My hands reach out and are clasped by larger hands. When I open my eyes, I see the smiling face of Cletus.

"Hello, NikkiMac, my sister and my friend." He wraps his arms around my shoulders and I start to cry like a baby.

"Hey, hey, what's wrong? Please don't cry! I thought you'd be glad to see me!"

Poppa Pace reassures Cletus, "Son, those are tears of relief and joy."

I try to pull myself together. "Cletus, you look so good! Praise God! I can look at your skin color and your eyes and see you've been taking care of yourself."

"If you mean drinking no alcohol, you're certainly right, NikkiMac. Thank you for finding me the day my mother died. Thank you for chasing after me and making sure I got help. God sent you to be my guardian angel that day, because I was truly at the beginning of a major relapse."

"Please sit down, both of you. Cletus, tell me what's been going on since I saw you last." Both men sit on the sofa. Cletus bows his head and takes a deep breath.

"Well, when my mother died, I used that as a reason to take a drink. One drink led to another, and that's why I was messed up when you saw me. I think I was trying to drink until I passed out and couldn't feel any more pain. NikkiMac, I truly loved my mother, even though it took me a long time to show her. At least she knew how I felt about her before she went to her rest."

"I know you loved her, Cletus, and I know you love the Lord, too." I resist the urge to hug him again, because I want to hear what else he has to say.

"I'm so thankful you took me to Brother Pace that day. He helped me gain the clarity to see that I had to get with God. I also had to get with my sponsor, so I could pull up before I sank too far and began to make more excuses for my slip. NikkiMac, I remember how it used to be when I was drinking. I don't ever want to live that way again. I'm powerless against alcohol; it's not my friend. God, my sponsor, and Brother Pace got me through the funeral arrangements, the private ceremony, and the adjustments that come with death. Day by day, I get stronger. My support network has grown larger, and I haven't had a drop of alcohol since you last saw me. Thank you from the bottom of my heart, NikkiMac." Poppa Pace nods his head in agreement, and Cletus continues. "I don't know what's going to happen with Angeleese, the children, and me. I've got to continue to hold on to the Lord and let Him guide me. I'm no good to her and the kids if I'm unsteady in my Christian walk. My feelings for her and the children still exist, that's why I plan to continue to be supportive of them. God will give me direction." I go in again to hug my brother, my friend. After our embrace, Cletus looks at Poppa Pace.

"Brother Pace, this isn't the first time in my life that you've helped me out, but what you did this time was crucial for my sobriety. You've stood by me since my relapse, without looking down on me. As a matter of fact, you've never looked down on me, even when I was out in the streets."

Poppa Pace puts his arm around Cletus' shoulder. "Son, as long as God gives me breath, I'll do what I can to help you on your way. We all have at least one demon to combat, and the Bible says we've all done wrong at some point in our lives. Just keep trying to do what's right, and God will help you, because He loves you. Welcome home, Cletus."

Chapter 26

Church Picnic

"You really miss Jacee, don't you, NikkiMac?" Anna Maria's beautiful blue eyes are full of concern as she hands the greeting card back to me. I put the card from Jacee back in its envelope before I answer.

"Of course I miss her. We've been best friends since we were children, practically inseparable, but this educational opportunity is perfect for her. I'd be selfish to deny her my support. Besides, she and I contact each other all the time, and she'll be back in Trenton before long. Anyway, Miss Anna Maria DelGrosso, you and I have pretty much formed a second dynamic twosome, haven't we?"

"So true, NikkiMac. We do hang out together a lot these days. I hope Jacee won't have a problem with it when she returns."

"The more true friends, the better. Come on, let's get inside the church building before service starts." We find our seats a few seconds before Brother Carlos opens service with a prayer and the scripture reading.

"Please turn in your Bibles to Romans chapter 12, verse 13, and follow along with me as I read out loud." Pages rustle, and then Brother Carlos reads. "Next, please turn to Hebrews chapter 13, verse 2." More pages turn. The ushers hand Bibles to visitors who came without them and church members help others find the verses in the Bible. There's no rush. We wait for those who want to read the scriptures for themselves to find the right place in their Bibles. "Our next scripture reading is First Peter chapter 4, verse 9. Let's all read this verse out loud." It sounds wonderful to hear the Bible read by the large group in the auditorium. Brother Carlos continues, "Each of these scriptures we just read are about hospitality, and what God requires of us concerning hospitality. This is our theme for this Sunday. And now, our minister will give more information about today's hospitality outreach."

Brother Johnson stands and speaks to us. "Good morning to you all! God has blessed us with a beautiful day. Amen?"

"Amen!" The group's positive response is robust.

"As you know, our first community picnic takes place today. We have a church picnic every year, but with this one we open up to our community. The Building Committee has done a wonderful job of preparing our churchyard. Many members of the congregation have generously prepared and donated food for the picnic. The Kitchen Committee has informed me that we have plenty of delicious food to share with our guests today. I'm so thankful that practically every member has invited one guest from the community to attend worship and then stay after service to enjoy our picnic. As I look out into the audience today, my heart is glad to see so many visitors. You visitors are our honored guests. If you have any questions about the worship service or about the Bible, please feel free to ask me after worship. I'm always happy to speak about God's plan of salvation. Now, Brother Vincent will come forward to lead us in song."

The sweet harmony of *When Morning Comes* rings out. We sing *Only In Thee*, and *There's A Crown For Your Cross*. As usual, Anna Maria's extraordinary soprano voice makes me think of heaven. I often wonder why she's so active in this congregation, yet not a member, but I'm glad she attends. When I check my watch, I note that fifteen minutes have passed since service began, and my guest, Martha, hasn't arrived. She's a woman I met during a door-to-door evangelism outreach effort with Brother Adam. Martha allowed us to come into her home on Dickinson Street. She listened attentively as we discussed the Bible and the church. I followed up with some phone calls to invite her, and she finally said she'd attend today. I'm a little disappointed, because I want to have a guest today and I want the guest to be Martha, someone from the neighborhood with whom I had a personal encounter.

"Good morning, Miss NikkiMac. I'm sorry I'm late. It took me forever to find a pair of stockings with no runs in them!" It's Martha.

"Oh, I'm so happy to see you! Please sit here next to me." Anna Maria moves over and Martha sits on the pew next to me. I signal the usher to bring me a visitor card so Martha can fill it out. She has her own

Bible, I notice. During communion, Martha reaches for the bread and the cup like an old pro. I see Anna Maria's eyebrows lift up at this, but I don't say a word. Anna Maria doesn't participate in the communion here, but she regularly bows her head while the brothers pray for the body and blood of Christ. It's begun to dawn on me that she makes the choices she makes when *she* believes she should. No one pressures or guilt trips Anna Maria about her decisions. After communion, Brother Vincent leads *Stepping In The Light* and *You Never Mentioned Him to Me*. Then, Brother Johnson walks to the podium.

"That's some mighty fine singing, church! You all make me really want to preach today!"

"Amen, Brother Johnson!"

"That's all right, brother! Preach!"

Brother Johnson laughs. "I know you want me to preach, but I also know you don't want me to preach too long, because you smell the mouth-watering feast outside, just like I do. The aroma of the picnic food calls me too, but the Bible tells us about the importance of our spiritual food, so let's first have our spirits fed. Am I right about it?"

"Amen!"

"That's right, brother!"

"In First Chronicles chapter 29, verse 14, David offers public praises to God. He and the people make generous donations to build the temple, but David recognizes that it's God who first gave to them, and His blessings allowed them to give for the building of the temple. This is the principle I emphasize today. Our loving and merciful heavenly Father gave everything we have to us. We should appreciate these benefits, and we should be willing to share these gifts and blessings with others. Our gifts from God, whether they're spiritual or physical, are not for us to grasp exclusively for ourselves. The Bible tells us to do good to all. Today, our goal is to be hospitable with our food and our fellowship. We also want to generously share the gospel with our guests who are interested, because we know the gospel is received by folks who are honestly seeking for truth."

As Brother Johnson continues to preach, I notice a man enter the auditorium and stand motionless by the doors. For some strange reason, he seems familiar, like from a long ago place, but I can't figure it out. At first, he doesn't look around for a particular church member, like an invited guest would. An usher leads him to a seat. He settles in, and then he looks around the room until our eyes lock. Quickly, I break eye contact and attempt to tune back into the service, but something inside me tenses for a moment.

"NikkiMac, aren't you going to stand for the invitation song?" Anna Maria alerts me. I try to shake off the weird feeling and join in singing *When I See The Blood*. My stomach starts to growl during the collection of the offering. It's because of all the delightful food smells. Thankfully, the announcements are brief. I close my eyes and think about Sister Carolina's creamy macaroni and cheese and Sister Lovey Grace's coconut cake with the pineapple filling. The next thing I know, our minister is about to make another announcement.

"Members who have guests, please make sure you escort them to the churchyard and introduce them to others. Don't rush to get yourselves some delicious food and leave our guests stranded in the churchyard. Look out for our company. Be hospitable. Amen?"

"Amen, Brother Johnson!" Brother Johnathan says a closing prayer, including a blessing of the food, and morning worship service is complete. We make our way outside, and the aromas from the grills make my mouth water. Anna Maria, Martha, and I find a spot at a picnic table, where I formally introduce them to each other.

"Your name is Anna Maria DelGrosso? Are you from this neighborhood?" asks Martha.

"No, but I grew up in Trenton, Martha. I work at the same school as NikkiMac." Anna Maria smiles warmly. By now, most of the church members have gotten used to seeing her at church services and events. This congregation has a majority of African American members, but there are also members from other ethnic groups. I watch Martha to see where she's coming from with her remarks, even though I know Anna Maria can handle herself.

"Martha, isn't it wonderful that God focuses on the heart and not the skin color or ethnicity?" Anna Maria asks.

"You're right, Anna Maria. I was thinking that you go to church here because you live in East Trenton. I didn't think this part of Trenton had Italian Americans still living in it, not like long ago when I moved here. That's all I meant."

"No offense taken, Martha. I worship here because I'm drawn to the truth of the Bible. I'll become a member one day." Martha opens her mouth to say more, but I step into the conversation.

"I don't know about you ladies, but the line for the fried whiting fish is starting to form, and I want to be near the front of it!" Anna Maria and Martha stop their exchange and follow me to the brother who works the large electric frying pan. On the way, we pass by the brother working the grill with the hot dogs and hamburgers and the brother working the grills with the ribs and chicken. The young children are in picnic paradise. They can't decide whether to eat food, or run, or drink cold drinks. The teenaged boys and girls try to act cool and eat while they innocently flirt in a way that won't draw the attention of the watchful adults. The weather is gorgeous and sunny. Suddenly, I feel arms encircle my waist from behind.

"Guess who, Sister NikkiMac?" I twist around and see Shaylonda's radiant face.

"Hello, Miss Shaylonda. It's great to see you. I wasn't sure you were here. We have so many people at church today that I must have overlooked you."

"Sister NikkiMac, say hello to my guest." Shaylonda's mother, Iris, reaches to give me a hug.

"Iris! I'm so pleased you're here. We've been keeping up with each other by phone, but you didn't tell me you were coming to church today."

"I wanted to surprise you, NikkiMac. I have to tell you again how much I appreciate what you did for my Shay and me. I respect the way you handled the situation. You could have ignored it or run and told everybody but me. I might not know a lot about the Bible, but as far as I understand it, you did what a Christian should do. I've been thinking seriously about connecting with this church because of the Christian care you gave my child. In fact, I'm meeting with Minister Johnson and his wife later today. I want to find out more about being added to the church."

My heart sings. "Iris, that's great news!"

Shaylonda interrupts. "Sister NikkiMac, we'll see you later. I want my mother to meet some more of my young church friends." They wave goodbye and head for a table of young people.

Suddenly, Martha points toward the rear of the churchyard and says, "NikkiMac, is that Mad Maggie standing with the church brother over there? I think she's waving at you." I look where Martha points. It's

Mad Maggie, and she is sort of smiling at me. Brother Adam Greene is with her. She must be his invited guest.

"As long as I've been in this neighborhood, I've never seen Mad Maggie smile and look pleasant like that. The man standing next to her must be a saint to have that kind of effect on her," Martha marvels. "Wait a minute, I remember him. He came to my house with you that day. That's Brother Greene, right?"

"That's correct, Martha. It's Brother Adam Greene, our assistant minister, and he does have a way with difficult people. I remember when he and I knocked on Mad Maggie's door during outreach evangelism. She didn't have one kind word for me, but she took a religious tract from him." I stop short of telling Martha more about the budding relationship between Adam and me. Anna Maria simply smiles. I wave back at Mad Maggie, but decide not to press my luck by walking over to start a friendly conversation with her. However, I do make a mental note to refer to her as Madilyn, her given name, from now on. After we get our fried fish, potato salad, macaroni and cheese, collard greens, cornbread, bottled water, and dessert, we settle in at our picnic table.

"This food is delicious, NikkiMac!" Anna Maria exclaims.

"Um, um, um!" Martha approves.

"Yes, yes, it's good enough to make a rabbit hug a hound!" I manage to get a few words out between my chews and finger licks.

Boopy, a neighborhood drunk, and a couple of his pals enter the churchyard. Brother Pace, Brother Sampson, and Brother Johnson notice. The three church brothers approach Boopy and his crew and speak with them. Then, Brother Sampson and Brother Pace lead Boopy and his pals to a table and point out the food lines. Boopy puts his raggedy book bag on the picnic table and then walks to get food with his pals. Brother Pace approaches our table.

"Hello, Daughter NikkiMac. Hello, Anna Maria." He and I give each other a hug, and Anna Maria greets him. He acknowledges Martha. "You must be one of our guests. Welcome, and I'm glad you're here with us today."

"Thank you. My name is Martha. NikkiMac invited me."

"Poppa Pace, why are Boopy and his friends allowed to be a part of this picnic? They didn't attend the worship service and they don't appear to be guests of any of our members. Besides, do you remember the last time he came inside the building? He brought a bottle of booze and tried to offer a swig to Cletus!"

"I know, Daughter NikkiMac. That's why we spoke with them before we agreed to let them stay. No one here invited them, but they're part of this community. They surely need Christian fellowship. Maybe some good will result from it. The brothers will keep an eye on them. Now, you relax and enjoy your meal. Make sure you introduce Martha to Sister Lovey Grace and some of the other church sisters and brothers. I'll check on you ladies in a little while." Before Poppa Pace can get far away, Brother Darius Muse slithers over. I don't see a visitor with him, and that doesn't surprise me.

"Good afternoon, lovely ladies." I don't know what else he says, because I tend to tune him out sometimes. I don't wish anything bad on him, but I still prefer him to stay out of my face. He knows why, even if he tries to play it off. Anna Maria introduces Martha to him. I turn my attention to the children at play, and I begin to walk around the churchyard to speak to other members and their guests. I hang out for a while with Cletus, Angeleese, and her children. They take up almost a full table. Plus, Cletus has a guest, as does Angeleese. Cletus really looks healthy and happy these days.

"NikkiMac, I'm clean and serene. Praise God." I give him a hug and start to walk away to visit at another table, but I hear him call me back.

"What's up, Cletus?"

His expression is cloudy. "NikkiMac, you won't believe this, but Boopy and his boys have broken out the red plastic cups with the white insides and rims. You know what that means, don't you?"

"Not really, Cletus, but that's odd, because we don't need cups. We're serving only water, iced tea, and juice in recyclable plastic bottles. Oh! Wait a minute! I know Boopy has better sense than to bring alcohol into this churchyard."

"He brought it into the church building once, didn't he?" Cletus frowns and gets up from the picnic table. I look around for Poppa Pace. He quickly notices this and approaches us.

"Daughter NikkiMac, what's wrong? Cletus?" I point, and before I can finish my sentence about Boopy and what's in the red plastic cups, Cletus, Brother Sampson, and Poppa Pace head for Boopy and his two cronies. The next thing I know, Boopy, his book bag, and his buddies are escorted from the churchyard. They have long faces, but they offer no physical resistance and they say nothing. Cletus rejoins Angeleese, their guests, and the children. Poppa Pace walks over to me.

"Daughter NikkiMac, thanks for bringing Boopy's antics to my attention. He had a bottle of whiskey and plastic cups in his book bag. He and his friends thought they were going to eat, drink whiskey, and chill out here today, but we let them know it wasn't happening. The devil's always busy, but we escorted that trio out in the name of the Lord." The sight of his mischievous smile amuses me.

"I know, Poppa Pace." I have to grin and shake my head as he walks over to one of the other picnic tables. I start to walk back to the table where Anna Maria, Martha and I first settled, and I notice that Brother Sampson and Anna Maria are at the table. They're involved in what looks like a friendly conversation. Martha is now at another table with Sister Sharlette Johnson, our minister's wife. When I get to the table with Brother Sampson and Anna Maria, they don't seem to notice me at first, so I interrupt.

"You two seem to be having a good time. I didn't know you knew each other that well." Anna Maria smiles and simultaneously flashes her gorgeous blue eyes at me. I think this is a message for me to mind my own business. That's not about to happen, because this should be fun.

"NikkiMac, I noticed something going on with Boopy a few minutes ago, so I asked Brother Sampson to come over and fill me in."

Brother Sampson offers, "That's correct, Sister NikkiMac. Since I was here, I formally introduced myself to your friend, Miss Anna Maria DelGrosso. I hope you don't mind." Did he just roll the "r" in her last name? Is he messing with me?

"Why would I have a problem with that, Brother Sampson? Isn't hospitality our objective for today?" We all chuckle at my cheeky response.

"Oh, by the way, Sister NikkiMac, have you had any more problems at your house since the possible intruder incident?"

"No, nothing else like that has happened. It must have been a dream. Maybe I *thought* I'd locked my back door, Brother Sampson. However, there are a couple of weird things: I couldn't find my ring box the morning after you officers came by and an unfamiliar car parked across the street from my house one night. Someone was in the car smoking a cigarette. My paranoia convinced me that a stranger was watching me. I told myself I was being silly, and I haven't noticed anything else odd or threatening since then. Thanks for checking on me, Brother Sampson."

"Glad to do it, my sister. Be sure to call me if you need me." He sounds upbeat, but both he and Anna Maria look a little troubled. Before Anna Maria can express her feelings, Brother Adam and his guest Madilyn join us. She has two large takeout containers of food.

"Well, Brother Greene and the rest of you, I'm gonna head on out now. The food's delicious, but it's too holy up in here for me. Thanks for inviting me, though." She fixes her mouth into her best version of a smile. I stifle a laugh when Anna Maria elbows me. Brother Sampson and Adam walk Madilyn to the gate.

"Anna Maria, she just came to feed her face!"

"Well, at least she came here, NikkiMac. But it is funny."

Brother Johnson announces over the sound system, "May I have your attention please? There's something special I want you all to witness." The crowd quiets, and Brother Johnson continues, "Will Brother Foster Pace and Sister Lovey Grace please come forward?" I think I know what's coming next, because as he walks by me on his way to Brother Johnson, Poppa Pace gives me a quick pat on the shoulder and a wink. The two Christians take their places before Brother Johnson, and the minister hands the microphone to Brother Pace. He looks tenderly at Sister Lovey. She wears her usual pleasant expression, but there's a slight question in her eyes.

"Sister Lovey, I have a something to ask you."

"What is it, Foster? Is it something everybody here needs to hear?" There's a buzz in the crowd. I think most of the women know what's about to go down.

Brother Pace looks like a nervous schoolboy as he reaches into his pocket, pulls out a ring box, opens it, and hands it to Sister Lovey Grace. "Sister Lovey, will you do me the honor of becoming my wife?" She glances at the ring. Then, she gazes at him in silence for a few seconds.

"Dear Foster, of course I'll marry you. What took you so long to ask?" They embrace. He places the engagement ring on her finger, and we all cheer. I think a couple of the single sisters almost swoon at the sight of something they deeply desire for themselves. I'm joyful for both Poppa Pace and Sister Lovey, even though this means I'll have to lean on him a lot less. It'll be okay."

"Praise God!" says Brother Johnson. "Marriage is truly honorable in His sight! It's a blessing that He's allowed these two faithful saints to find one another. Now, they want to make a commitment in marriage."

"Hallelujah!"

"Praise Him!"

"Amen!"

The women crowd around Sister Lovey to offer their best wishes and support. The men crowd around Brother Pace to congratulate him. The children run around in circles just because they can. Angeleese cries tears of joy. She probably longs for the time when she and Cletus have their moment like this. I believe it'll happen, if it's God's will. There's a good spirit over this place. A little while later, we start to wind down. Brother Johnson says a closing prayer and invites our guests to return for worship next Sunday and Bible classes this coming week. The brothers extinguish the grill fires, and the committee members and some of the rest of us start the cleanup.

"NikkiMac, I'm going to walk home, but you don't have to come with me. I had a wonderful time today. Thank you for inviting me. I plan to return soon." Martha appears cheerful, yet pensive.

"Martha, I'm so glad you accepted my invitation. Remember to call the number on the tract I gave you if you have any questions. You have an open invitation here." She waves and walks away. Then, Anna Maria breezes by with an announcement.

"NikkiMac, Brother Sampson's going to take me home, so you don't have to go all the way across town." I chuckle and resist the urge to tell her that she's never minded before about me driving all the way across town to take her home.

"I need to say something to you before you leave, NikkiMac." It's Adam. Now what? This is a Sunday of surprises.

"I'm finished with my cleanup tasks, Adam. What's on your mind?"

"You and I haven't been able to spend much time together, even though I told you a while back that I was going to work on that. It's been on my mind, NikkiMac, so I made a conscious effort to wrap up some of my work projects. Why don't we set aside Friday nights, starting with this coming Friday, as our Date Nights? Let's take this time to learn more about each other, away from church services or church projects. We can explore what this Christian preacher man and this Christian teacher woman can become to each other. We'll never know if we don't take the time to find out. Am I right?" He smiles at me. His expression is gentle.

I'm so fixed on Adam that I can't give him an immediate response. Suddenly, I'm afraid that if I get to spend more time with this godly and appealing man, desire may rise in me. With my history before I became a Christian, do I deserve such a faithful man, a man who's a minister, no less? What if I ruin what God may have planned for Adam and me?

Just before I go further into these thoughts, I remember a verse in the book of Proverbs, and it calms me down. I'm going to trust God fully, and not myself, because He'll guide my steps. All I have to do is allow Him to lead me.

Now, I've got an answer. "You're right, Adam. Let's take the time to find out."